THE DELICIOUS DOLLS

had Rod Damon—The Coxeman—limp with exhaustion.

Invited by the Red Chinese to test his famed virility against the wildest women in the inscrutable East—Rod finds that he's just not up to it. The dolls have done him in!

But then Rod's agile brain smells a switch, and he stumbles onto the weirdest sex secret in the annals of international hanky-panky.

A secret so devastating that even Rod isn't sure he can handle the consequences . . .

Other Books In This Series

By Troy Conway

THE BLOW YOUR MIND JOB

JUST A SILLY MILLIMETER LONGER

THE BIG BROAD JUMP

I'D RATHER FIGHT THAN SWISH

A GOOD PEACE

WHATEVER GOES UP

HAD ANY LATELY?

IT'S WHAT'S UP FRONT THAT COUNTS

THE BEST LAID PLANS

THE MAN-EATER

KEEP IT UP, ROD

LAST LICKS

COME ONE, COME ALL

IT'S GETTING HARDER ALL THE TIME

THE WHAM! BAM! THANK YOU,
MA'AM AFFAIR

THE BILLION DOLLAR SNATCH

THE BIG FREAK-OUT

THE BERLIN WALL AFFAIR

COXEMAN #18

THE SEX MACHINE

AN ADULT NOVEL BY BY TROY CONWAY

POPULAR LIBRARY

Popular Library
Hachette Book Group USA
237 Park Avenue
New York, NY 10017

Popular Library is an imprint of Grand Central Publishing. The Popular Library name and logo is a trademark of Hachette Book Group USA, Inc. The Coxeman name and logo is a trademark of Hachette Book Group USA, Inc.

Visit our Web site at www.HachetteBookGroupUSA.com

First Paperback Printing: January, 1970

Printed in the United States of America

Conway, Troy
Sex Machine, The / Troy Conway
(Coxeman, #18)

ISBN 0-446-54330-6 / 978-0-446-54330-9

CHAPTER ONE

The women bore down on me in a squealing, screeching line. There is something terrifying about a mob of women—there must have been hundreds of them—descending on you at the gallop, yelling their delight at sight of your face. Famous people will know what I mean, movie stars and all that, pop singers, Frank Sinatra and The Beatles.

Me, I was no movie star.

I paled visibly and reached out for support. I caught hold of Miss Angela Montosores, the advertising representative of Blake, Bannister and Hadshaw, my publishers. I had written a book entitled *The Sex Machine*, and now I was paying the penalty of its being on the best-seller list one week after publication.

"Help me," I moaned.

Her dark eyes danced gleefully. "Why, Professor Damon! Women are your speciality. Your book is going to break all records for sales."

The women reached me, grabbed for my tie, my coat and its buttons, even for my pants. I tried to laugh as I put my arms about two of them. A pair of soft, moist lips jammed against my mouth. Involuntarily I kissed them and found my tongue being gently bitten between a set of teeth. Perfume and silk and soft flesh was all around me so that I floated in a sea of sensuality and squealing sexpots.

I had no idea this would happen when I began *The Sex Machine*. Maybe I would never have written it if I'd been gifted with foreknowledge. Or maybe I would. I am a professor of sociology and the founder of the League for Sexual Dynamics at the university. It always enhances the reputation and earning power of a college professor to write a book or two. This was mine. In it I was passing on to an eager public the vast sexual know-how I have acquired with the women of five continents.

In my book I teach men and women how to have a good time with each other. It is a primer for phallic expertise. I include a virility diet for husbands and playboys. I slip in amorous asides to my female readers, telling them how to make sure their husbands and lovers can best maintain *karezza*—that power to prolong the act indefinitely—which they all seek.

I am gifted with *karezza* by nature, since I suffer—if *suffer* is the word—from satyriasis. *Coitus prolongatus* is a way of life with me. I can enjoy multiple, complete orgasms. This is fine for pasonamiac play—pasonomia being the condition in which one is interested in all forms of sexual intercourse—but it does have a strange effect on the women whom I bed down.

They exhaust themselves trying to make up bizarre ways to expel male juice. This makes for very interesting results, and more than once has helped me in my role of secret agent for the Thaddeus X. Coxe Foundation. But my case is unique. In my book, I address myself to most men and most women. The majority rules, especially in a sex tome.

I wrote of foreplay and flirtation, of pleasure plateaus and phallic inventiveness, of prolongation, of aftermath and response. Mine was the one definitive book on human sex relationships. I told it all and I told it the way it really is.

Mainly, however, *The Sex Machine* teaches people to psyche themselves into being great lovers. The sex act is very much a product of the mind, of the mental attitude. And the minds of our western men and women have been so conditioned by the puritanical attitudes of the early settlers and colonists that they still regard the sex act as somehow sinful. I am sure that many of them subconsciously blame God for not having created man and woman in a form that would do away with the need for sex relations to have a child.

To overcome this tendency to think of sex as sin, I devote many chapters in my book, explaining that good health and a liking for rollicking sex go hand in hand, and that a man or a woman can achieve this marvelous balance of health and loving by talking himself into it, by psyching himself into overcoming the puritanical repressions of his environment and bringing-up.

In my mind it is the most important part of it.

It sets *The Sex Machine* apart from all other sex manuals.

I tell it as it is.

Judging by these females around me—jumping and jerking against me, squealing and sighing—I had told it very well indeed. I could hear Angela Montosores begging them to be patient and to line up for me to autograph their copies. She was ignored, thrust aside to the perimeter of the mob.

I had to quell this uprising by my lonesome.

I grabbed a handful of black hair and used it to boost myself upward. I planted a foot on a thigh and hoisted my body until I could transfer my other foot to a shoulder. The women were laughing, weeping, clapping their hands in mass hysteria. I got my other foot up so that I towered over them, standing on two different shoulders.

They stared up at me with adoring eyes, as if I were the sex god, the Shiva or Baal their excited little minds were making out of me.

"Ladies," I began.

They squealed. I lifted my hands. They quieted.

"One at a time." I smiled down at them. "We'll never get anywhere carrying on like this."

"Give us a sample," somebody cried.

Angela Montosores was blushing and making signs with her hand as she peered at me from the edge of the crowd. I glanced down. My fly had come open, the zipper tugged down by some overenthusiastic hand. No wonder the girls were going wild. I pulled up the zipper and tried to restore order.

"Do we have a private room where I can speak with each lady?" I called to Angela.

The desk and chair had been set up in a corner of the store, away from the other shoppers. The desk was piled high with copies of THE SEX MACHINE for those who had their twenty-dollar bills handy, and lacked a copy. The store had set up this publicity arrangement. Now that publicity gimmick was backfiring on it. I could see a couple of horrified floorwalkers and an assistant manager or two standing in the aisles, their eyes bulging.

I jumped down, saying, "All right, ladies, this way."

I grabbed Angela Montosores by the arm. "A private room. Get me a private room with a desk and a chair in it. Otherwise, we're going to have a riot."

She looked dazed. Never in her wildest dreams had she ever been confronted with a situation like this.

"Y-yes, I g-guess so," she nodded.

She ran ahead of me, making frantic motions at an assistant manager. The women were all around me, and the crowd was getting bigger. I began to curse the day I'd begun writing my hints to needy females. Since some of the book was partly my own memoirs, in which I discussed love methods and habits around the world, and hot women I have known (without mentioning names), it was easy to see why these dames looked on me as a combination of Casanova and Don Juan.

Those boys are dead. I was here, in the flesh.

The assistant manager and Angela Montosores conferred. Then the girl turned and waved an arm, began racing off toward a different corner of the store. Behind her the assistant manager made signals at a couple of long-haired, young male stock clerks gawking at me with open mouths and envious eyes.

The women sensed I was about to grant them each a private interview. They squealed even more shrilly and hurried me along until my feet were barely touching the floor. I saw a green baize curtain. I was pushed against it, the curtain flew off to one side, and then I was standing in a little room not much larger than those cubicles men enter when they are buying a new suit, to put it on for tailoring.

There was a desk in the room, and a straight-backed chair. I don't know how they had done it so fast, but there were a number of copies of my book on top of the desk beside a ball-point pen. I drew a deep breath. Angela Montosores peeped in at me, past the green baize curtain.

"Ready?" she caroled.

"As I ever will be. Send the first lady in."

I sat down on the chair and reached for a pen. The curtain swished and a pretty little housewife came running in, yanking up her skirt. I did a double-take. She had quite good legs in beige stockings, and garters from a girdle clasping them. The skirt went up above the pink girdle.

"Ma'am, now look——"

"Oh, come on!" she squealed. Her hand tossed a crumpled twenty-dollar bill down on the desk. "Sign a book! But first —"

Her hand went to my zipper. Then it was burrowing inside my open fly, seizing upon my manhood. It was limp but her hot little hand did things and when the hand came out of the fly with its prisoner, her lipsticked mouth made a round wet O and she breathed, "Oooooooh!"

"Lady, this meeting was for the purpose of—"

She lifted a shapely leg and put it over my thighs. She beamed down at me, her lips slightly open.

"You wonderful man," she panted. "You're all a human male should be. I just want to see if you're everything your book says you are!"

She sank down slowly, taking me all in. She gave a soft cry and her girdled hips lurched. Then she was posting up and down like an accomplished horsewoman.

"Don't tell me all the others are as curious as you?"

She kept her eyes closed as she talked, but she let go of her lower lip. She had clenched it between her teeth.

"Certainly, darling. The whole kit and kaboodle of them. Why else do you think we're here? Oooooh, don't talk, just go on being the big darling you are and—oh! Oh! Oh!"

I thought she might call it a day after peaking so marvelously, but she got right back into the saddle and went off on her rantum-scantum ride again. Once she said, "I'm a little disappointed in you. I thought you knew some extra little tricks that would increase my pleasure. All you do is sit there."

It came to me that I was a public figure, with fans. I could not fail them, I told myself. I ran my palms along her soft bare thighs above her stockings. I slid one hand inward along her upper thigh and my fingernail scratched.

"Oh, yes! Oh, yes! Oh, yes!" she wailed.

"I haven't begun yet," I told her. "If you want to sample some of the love mysteries of the Orient, there is always the Persian method of *awurd-o-burd*, in which the male aids the enjoyment of the female by. . . ."

My words trailed off. My finger had found her clitoris hard and fairly long. I caressed it; I lavished upon it a cascade of caresses. The lady went crazy, bucking and bumping. She began to weep real tears and her mouth was wide open in a silent scream.

I glanced at my wristwatch. "I can't spare you much more time, my dear. It's after three and there are others who—"

She shut me up by gluing wet, wide lips to my mouth. We went on and on. I was having a ball, I admit. Most authors don't get this kind of reaction to their books and I was human enough to enjoy it. There was a nagging worry about the rest of the women, however. If I had to service each one of them *ad infinitum*, if I had to prove to each individual reader that the memoirs parts of my book were not all lies, I would be here forever.

There are more than a million women in this city. If only half of them were to buy my book and demand a personal proof of my abilities as a lover, I would be busy until——

"Professor Damon!" cried a voice.

I looked at the curtain where Angela Montosores had thrust her pretty face with the tumbled-down mop of thick brown hair atop her shapely skull. Her red mouth was wide open, and her eyes bulged. Then a couple more faces came into view. The other women registered jealousy, lust, rut-heat, anxiety, and impatience.

"Lady," I said. "There are others who——"

"Up theirs!" my love-mate screeched.

She was insatiable. She just could not get enough of this. Her leg muscles tightened and loosed as she went up and down on her toes, her thighflesh rippled and shook, her hips went back and forth, up and down and sideways.

I wondered if she knew we had an audience. I whispered, "The others are watching, lady."

"Let them! They're seeing a girl get banged in a dozen different directions. You got any more tricks?"

Of course I did, but I was not going to tell her that. She was being very selfish, and the sooner she learned the goodies were not exclusively her own, the better for everyone concerned.

A bell rang somewhere in the store.

"That's the warning signal, Professor Damon," yelled Angela Montosores. "The store closes in five minutes."

"We'll stay," screamed the ladies.

"Me too," echoed my tireless partner, still bumping and grinding away.

"How about tomorrow?" I said.

My housewifely doll opened her eyes wide. "Tomorrow? You'll be here tomorrow?"

"I'll be here for a month, looks like," I muttered.

I was enjoying myself! I'd be a cock-eyed liar if I said I wasn't. But the man likes to have some say as to when and where he sheathes his saber. Being attacked and semi-raped like this is not my idea of perfect pump thunder. I felt like the old Roman god, Mutunus Tutunus, on whose wooden member Roman brides used to sacrifice their virginity on their wedding nights.

Another bell begin to ring.

"Professor Damon," called Angela Montosores. "I'll call the guards. Really, you must pull yourself together. I want to go home."

"I know, baby. So do I."

She glared at me. I had to do something drastic. My free hand slid below the girdle, toward the bare buttock cheeks of my partner. I readied my middle finger. I drove it home.

The woman screamed and collapsed.

I pushed her off, but I supported her with an arm about her middle. "Give me a hand here," I called to Angela.

The Spanish girl ran in, reaching for me with quivering fingers. "Not there," I yelled, pushing her hand aside. "With her! Get her presentable, get her out of here. And then sneak me out, too."

Angela yanked down the woman's skirt, nodding. "Yes, yes. We'll get all the women out, then we'll go home, Professor."

I sank back into the chair as Angela led away the dazed darling. The other females oohed and aahed. I half expected them to push their way in and take what I had to offer, but the store managers finally discovered a way to manage a crisis like this. The uniformed guards made a flying wedge and though I heard the sounds of slaps and grunts, they got the women out of the store.

I stared at the copies of my book and snarled.

I could not take this, day after day. Or could I? Physically, yes. I am a veritable Hercules when it comes to heating the meat. It was my psyche that was tired at the moment. Man needs a rest at times, even from what he does best.

I put myself to order and stood up.

I walked out of the room into a deserted store. The lights were going off, one by one. Beyond the big front windows, snowflakes were starting to fall. It was a cold winter night, the weather forecast was for snow flurries, and the wind was damn chilly, cutting through my topcoat and my Pierre Cardin suit. I shivered as I eased myself out a door.

The women were gone, I guess the cold weather had put a damper on their rut heat. At any rate, I was alone and unbothered. I pulled the collar of my topcoat up around my jawline to hide my face.

"Psssst! Professor—this way," a voice hissed.

It was Angela Montosores, leaning an arm through the open window of a white Mustang and waving it at me. I wanted no part of Angela Montosores, but she had driven me from my apartment just off the university campus, and it was a long walk home. I grinned weakly and moved toward her car, seeing a white Camaro right behind her, waiting for her to move.

She was all smiles and bright eyed, with a length of nyloned leg showing where her mini-skirt was pulled back. I saw the glitter of a garterclasp as I slipped into the bucket seat beside her.

"Your place or mine?" she bubbled.

"Mine," I growled darkly. I wanted to sleep in my own bed tonight. Besides, I wanted the comfort of familiar surroundings.

"Shall we stop for food?" she asked, maneuvering the roadster in and out of traffic. She was wearing some expensive perfume I think was Chantilly. As she moved her legs, I saw the mini-skirt slip back to show a bare, dusky thigh. I looked away, remembering my pooped psyche.

"I can cook well."

"That was the greatest, what happened today," she went on, shifting gears and hitting the accelerator to avoid an oncoming truck. I sat speechless in the suicide seat, waiting for the crash.

The Mustang eased by the huge Mack. I got my breath back and began living again. She was barreling along the highway now, hitting sixty, nudging up toward seventy.

Gaily she said, "You'll make a fortune, honest. I've done some publicity for authors before, but you're way off by yourself. I read your book, I found it fascinating, although—"

Her voice trailed off dubiously. My authorial instincts aroused, I muttered, "Although—what? You seem to have some doubts about what I wrote. Be more specific."

"We-ell, that part about impotence and frigidity being only in the mind. You say it's just a psychosis based on environmental factors. I'm not so sure of that."

"It's true, all the same. Most men and women suffer from a personal guilt complex—their own or others—which prevents them from enjoying the genital goodies of life. I call it the *prohibitive psyche.*"

"I remember that. Yes. But you go on to suggest that the reader can overcome this *prohibitive psyche* by concentrating on it. Is that really, really true? Not just some gimmick to sell books? The flyleaf says any reader of your book, and practitioner of your advice, can make himself into a perfect Casanova. If it's a female, she can be a regular Messalina, no matter what her feelings toward sex now are."

"Correct. One can very easily psyche himself or herself into becoming a lady-killer or a red-hot mamma."

"I don't believe it," she said flatly.

Sure, I took the bait. I turned in my seat and stared at her profile. She was a Spanish girl, with the sultry features and lips of those who possess Castilian blood in their veins. Her body was lush, with quite generous breasts bloating out the bodice of the plain brown A-line dress she was wearing, and even her light topcoat. Her legs were fleshy, very shapely, and her hips rounded out her skirt with sensuous honesty.

"You could be a regular Cleopatra," I muttered.

She flashed me a big smile, but shook her head. "No. I'm too prim. I was brought up by strict parents and went to a school where I was taught by nuns. The lessons I was taught have scarred my psyche too thoroughly. I believe that sex is something a woman should have only with her husband, and then only to get children."

"You're kidding," I said dazedly. "Does anybody still feel like that these days?"

"I do."

"You don't think sex is fun?"

She shook her head. Her lips pursed almost primly as she said, "That exhibition you put on with—with that lady in the room at the store was disgusting."

"But you were fascinated by it," I accused.

"Well, yes. But only because it was quite unbelievable." She turned her head and looked at me contritely. "Please don't think there's anything personal in this. It's just that I'm quarreling with your ideas, not with you. And please don't tell my bosses about this discussion. You might get me fired."

"I'll consider you one of my pupils in my League for Sexual Dynamics classes. I get all kinds in there, even girls like you." I smiled at her, feeling somewhat better. "They're afflicted with puritanism too, with the doctrines handed down by sex-haters like Saint Paul."

She parked the Mustang, pulling it to one side of the road in front of a luxury food shop. "I really am curious. I'd give anything to be convinced that you're right. But I know you aren't. However, we can't argue on empty stomachs, so I'm going to make you some of my paella y sangria."

I followed her into the food market and reached for my wallet as she bought pork loin and chicken breasts, veal and sausage, livers and scallops, olive oil, pimentos, shrimps, mushrooms and saffron powder. There were a couple of other ingredients, but I don't remember them.

The bill came to twenty dollars.

"This better be good," I muttered.

Her bright smile flashed. "It will be. I always think better over food and drink. And I want you to explain your theories to me quite thoroughly."

As we were moving down the road to my pad, which is in a remote little corner of the university town—it's a swank condominium, I must admit—Angela Montosores began to speak. Her voice was low and controlled, but I did detect an undercurrent of anxiety, maybe even worry.

"You see," she began, "I'm a married woman living apart from her husband. To be honest about it, we're getting a divorce. Mike and I never really hit it off big—in bed. I—I was a timid virgin when he married me. I'm still timid, even if I'm no longer a virgin."

Her face was very brave; she was fighting tears.

"The first night we had relations, he was very considerate. I was frozen up inside. I was terrified of sex. I thought it was disgusting and indecent. I've been to school with nuns as teachers, and some of their beliefs rubbed off on me, rather much. I loved Mike, and maybe I still do. I don't know. But when he got into bed with me naked, something tightened up all inside me. It was all I could do to open my legs. Physically, I mean."

"Frigidity. It isn't uncommon," I murmured.

"I d-don't blame Mike, you understand," she added hastily.

The white Camaro I had seen outside the department store was behind us again, moving at our pace. Up ahead there was a woods, the road cutting between the trees and along a rocky gorge. I began to feel prickles down my neck. In my role as a special investigator for the Thaddeus X. Coxe Foundation, I get hunches every so often.

Angela was talking again. "I tried to be a good wife to him; I really did. I wanted to be good in bed for him. I just couldn't. That's why I'm so anxious to hear you discuss your views. I'm hoping you can convince me."

The Camaro was making its move. It was coming up fast on the outside lane, as if to pass us. There was no reason to suspect the two men seated in the bucket seats. They were well-dressed and appeared to be no more than businessmen on their way home from work.

"Angela—that car," I said.

"I see it. It's just passing. I'll give it more room."

She pulled the Mustang to the right. The Camaro followed it, almost scraping fenders. The Spanish girl cried out harshly in vexation.

"What's the matter with them? They're—ohhh!"

The fender grated. It was obvious even to Angela Montosores that the Camaro was forcing her off the road. She fought the wheel as the tires bumped on the rough edge of the road. Then the Mustang was tilting, sliding into a ditch, making for the trees flanking this corner of the highway.

"Professor! Rod—what are they doing?"

I didn't know, but it was for real. I caught a glimpse of two hard faces and the flash of light on the barrel of a revolver. As a Coxeman, I sometimes go armed, but I was just Professor Rod Damon at the moment, so I was as clean of hardware as a priest. I bounced around on the suicide seat and cursed under my breath.

"You got any enemies?" I grated.

"None! Have—"

Her last word was lost as her neck bounced when she applied the brakes. The car bumper stopped inches from a big tree looming up in the headlights. I reached for the door handle and was out of the Mustang and standing in the underbrush seconds later.

I wasn't fast enough. One of the two men was out of the Camaro ahead of me, aiming his gun in my direction. He was a big, bulky man with muscled arms and shoulders that strained the cloth of his big-checked sports jacket.

"Easy, Professor. Just don't move."

I stood waiting, my every muscle tensed. Apparently he was not out to murder me, because he had a clear shot at me. There was less than twenty feet between us and he had the look of a man used to firing guns.

"Tell your lady friend to stay here until we've gone," he rasped.

I did like he told me, not being a complete idiot. Then his gun barrel waggled and I walked toward him slowly. I came to a stop before him. His ham-like hand ran over my pockets, patting them lightly to make sure I was not carrying a gun.

"Into the car. The rear seat.

I got into the Camaro, squeezing into the narrow back seat. I was looking at Angela Montosores, seeing her stricken face peering at me. I made my lips smile encouragement at her, so as not to frighten her more than she was already frightened. Then I slid down into the back seat.

My thigh touched something soft. I turned and saw a girl smiling at me. She was a blonde, with long golden hair done up in a knot on top of her head. Her features were damn near perfect, and her mouth was a red fruit, slightly pouting. She wore a cashmere sweater with nothing but herself under it, and a plaid mini-skirt that gave me a look at all of her stockinged legs.

"Hello," she said with a sultry undertone.

"Hello yourself," I greeted her. "Who are you and what's this all about?"

The man with the revolver slammed the door shut and turned to me, letting me see the Savage .38. "Just be good, Professor, and you'll enjoy what's going to happen to you."

"Oh? What's that?"

The girl giggled. The man said, "You're going to make love to Cassie there until she gets tired of it—or until you die of exhaustion."

It was the nicest death sentence I'd ever heard.

CHAPTER TWO

The Camaro pulled away from the Mustang where Angela Montosores was still sitting, making no effort to start her stalled engine. I glanced back at her through the rearview mirror, seeing her face white and pinched in the cold moonlight.

The snow had stopped; it had never been much more than flurries, but the ground on either side of the road was white, and the trees were rimmed in what appeared to be white enamel. Wintertime is a cold, cruel time of year, and I felt its bite as I sat beside the blonde babe, wondering why I had been selected to do the honors.

"Was it because of my book?" I asked suddenly.

"What book?" asked the blonde.

"Don't talk, Cassie. Just sit there," said the driver.

The gunman chuckled. "Sort of, Professor. You've added to your reputation with that *Sex Machine*. Up until now, you've kind of been unknown—except to some of us in the spy game—but now you've gone and made yourself world famous."

"I'm regretting it already," I said honestly.

"Sorry about taking you away from your lady friend, but Cassie there will make you forget her. Cassie is a sexpot, Professor."

I turned to her, aware that the car was turning off the main road and moving up a slight hill onto a private drive that lead back to the heights of Mountain View. There was only one habitation up here, a posh summer resort called Sheffield Inn. The inn was closed for the winter, but in summertime it boasted a pool, a nine-hole golf course, and a view of the surrounding countryside that was worth the thirty dollars a day you paid for a room. There was local talk that the owners were considering turning the Sheffield into a ski resort, but there had been no action on the project.

"There's nothing up this way," I pointed out.

"Stop fretting, Professor. We rented the Sheffield. It has heat, you know, and very spacious accomodations for a party of four."

"I hope one of the party can cook," I hinted.

"No food, no drink. Just love."

The gunman gave an evil chuckle.

"But why?" I wondered.

"Just look on it as a compliment to your reputation."

I mulled that over. To my reputation as a cocksman—or a Coxeman? They were too radically different ideas, though one often went hand in hand with the other on my assignments. I decided the man was right. I would worry when it came time to worry. Right now I might as well sit back and enjoy the ride.

The Camaro braked to a stop in the otherwise empty parking lot, close by the fieldstone and glass walls of the inn lobby. Dim lights were on behind the thick glass panes. I could see the registry desk, the carpeted floor, the potted plants and the modernistic furniture. There was a huge stone fireplace, where a fire had been built against the wintertime cold.

The gunmen got out first. His gun wagged and I followed suit. The blonde came after me. Her hand slipped into mine. Her flesh was surprisingly warm. Well, the man had hinted that she was a hot number. Her fingernail tickled the palm of my hand. I gripped her finger in the accepted answer to such an invitation and squeezed it. She beamed.

The driver went ahead of us, unlocking the glass doors and holding them open so we could enter. The blonde slipped past me, brushing my chest with her sweatered breasts and affording me a fine view of her shifting buttocks under the plaid mini-skirt.

At any other time and under different circumstances, I could hardly have waited to get this pussycat between the sheets. She was a real joy wagon. She exuded sexuality as she did her female perfumes. Her lovely face turned to flash me a smile over her shoulder, and there was challenge and invitation in her blue eyes.

"Room one, Professor—the bridal suite," said the gunman.

The Sheffield Inn was built outward on three sides from the immense stone and glass lobby, in plush rooms radiating outward from the lobby. There was a cocktail lounge, a rather large dining room, a small reading room, and a row of small shops where the guests could buy expensive little items like French, or Jensen crystal, Gorham silver, books, magazines and assorted candies. These stores were dark now.

The bridal suite was at the end of the main corridor, separated from the other rooms by a breezeway, I suppose for the purpose of giving any newlyweds who might inhabit it a sensation of aloneness. I followed the twitching buttocks of my blonde bedmate down the carpeted hall.

I did not intend to go through with this kidnap knee-trembler caper. I like my loving, but I like also to pick and choose my partners. This doll I was following was eminently erotic, but I wanted none of her.

The only trouble was, I didn't know how to get out of it. My mind raced like a Challenger going down the Utah salt flats, but it couldn't kick up any escape ideas. And time was running short. The gunman was right at my heels, his Savage ready in his hand.

Once I was inside the bridal suite, he would post himself outside the door, probably on a chair, to stand guard. Inside the room I would be forced to perform for the enjoyment of the blonde. I gathered that if her embraces didn't kill me, the man would. He would lock me into the rooms. When he unlocked that door, only one of us was supposed to come out, and it wouldn't be me.

Now understand me. I was not afraid of a blanket horn pipe with this Cassie. My priapism would not let me be defeated by a woman in the love lists. I have jousted with too many females not to know this. Once I went into that room with the blonde, I would overcome her apparent nymphomania and knock her cold with exhaustion. But this wasn't enough. She was supposed to kill me with erotic kindness, and it just couldn't be done.

So then the gunman would shoot me.

He flashed a grin as the blonde opened the door. "So long, Professor," he chuckled. "What a way to go!"

Out of the corner of my eye I saw that Cassie was lifting the sweater up over her head, arms crossed in front of her. Her naked pink back was perfect, soft and shapely.

The gunman let his eyes slide to all that flesh.

My right hand moved, blurring. The edge of my hand hit his gun-wrist, driving it sideways. At the same moment my right knee came up between his legs, hard. He opened his mouth and his eyes glazed a moment. It was all the time I needed. My left hand chopped at his throat, ramming into his Adam's apple. His head went back.

I tore the gun from his lax fingers, drove the barrel into his solar plexus. As the wind went out of him, I pulled the trigger.

Cassie was staring at me from the bedroom, naked above the belt of her plaid mini-skirt. My subconscious registered the fact that she had gorgeous breasts. My subconscious mind was not on breasts at the moment, but on the driver of the Camaro.

I whirled. The driver was yelling, coming down the hall at me. The Savage bucked in my hand and the driver crumpled, dropping to the carpeted hallway and sliding into the wall. He was dead when his body stopped moving, my bullet had caught him smack in the mouth.

I swung on the girl. She was still standing there, without any expression on her lovely face other than that smile of challenge and invitation. As I watched, she undid her belt and, bending forward, slid her mini-skirt downward. She must have seen me shoot her two companions, but she acted as if all she had on her mind was the bit of belly bumping I was supposed to perform with her.

I said brightly, "Honey, go get into the sheets."

She nodded happily, straightening and dropping the mini-skirt to a nearby chair. She was really something in her beige stockings and white garterbelt. Her mound was shaven clean of hair so that her feminine dimple was very obvious. At another time—

I pulled myself together. I was going to have to report this caper to Walrus-moustache, my chief in the Coxe Foundation. He was going to have to get me out of a homicide charge. I figured I could beat the rap, I had been kidnapped; but I wanted reassurance.

My hand pulled the bridal suite door toward me. There was a key in the lock, with which the gunman intended to lock me in with my doom date. I turned the lock and withdrew the key, putting it into my pocket.

Then I ran.

The ignition key was still in the Camaro. I turned it, revved the motor, backed up and wheeled the car down the long, winding driveway. I wanted back with Angela Montosores, and then I wanted home to the safety of my pad.

To my delight, the Mustang was still there.

Angela was crying a flood of tears, head bent over the steering wheel. I braked the Camaro and ran for her. At the sound of my voice, her face came up into the winter moonlight.

"Can you start the car?" I rasped.

"Oh! You got away! What did——"

"Never mind the conversation. Let's get the hell out of here. I've got to make a telephone call."

She nodded. The Mustang motor purred to life and she backed up onto the road, narrowly missing the Camaro where I'd left it. Then, straightening her wheels, she shot off down the road. She was still sniffling, so I took my handkerchief out of my pocket and wiped her eyes.

"It's all right," I soothed. "It was all a mistake."

"I'm not used to violence," she spluttered.

"Neither am I," I lied. "They listened to my arguments by which I convinced them they had the wrong patsy."

My arguments had been .38 bullets, but I didn't tell her that. I wondered about the blonde. She might rouse up the police in short order once she got out of the locked room. If she got out, that is. I doubted it. Somebody would have to go and free her, but it wouldn't be me.

Angela Montosores slid the Mustang into the parking lot beside my own car, at the moment a Coup de Ville. The Ashford Arms, where I had my apartment, was a recent addition to the architecture around the university town. It was for reasonably well-to-dos, some of them married, some still bachelors like myself. It cost a lot, but I was making good money at the university, what with my sociology courses and my League for Sexual Dynamics studies, and I had my income as a Coxeman to add to it. So I indulged myself.

My pad was on the second floor. I opened the blue metal door, flicked on a wall switch, and stood back. Angela Montosores oohed, her dark eyes shining. Her red-nailed fingers clasped themselves at her front and her lips fell open.

"It's a picture out of *Playboy,*" she breathed rapturously.

"I do like the good things of life," I admitted.

There was wall-to-wall cotton shag carpeting in beige, holding metal-framed Van Keppel-Green lounges and chairs, a KLH stereo system, wooden walls rising to a high ceiling, a mahogany bar that separated from the rest of the room the cookerie where I could scramble up some eggs and ham for late night snacks. There were four cushioned stools in front of the bar proper, and a glass shelf display of bottles behind, that opened into the kitchen on the far side. Ferns and cactus in brass pots and barrels added a kind of outdoorsy look to the whole place.

Angela stalked into my lair like a tigress, letting her hips swing. It was almost as if she was a completely different girl in these posh surroundings. She pulled down her bodice and lifted her skirt, giving me a glimpse of breastflesh and dusky thighmeat.

She whirled, doing a little pirouette. "I love it. It's absolutely perfect. I—I think I'm even going to have a drink."

I carried the packages of food out into the kitchen. Apparently she had forgotten the paella y sangria she was supposed to cook for me. I dumped the groceries on the chopping block of grained wood that was a part of the kitchen counters, and went back behind the bar.

I made martinis and served them in frosted glasses just out of the freezing unit of the bar refrigerator. I dropped tiny onions into each one.

"To the furthering of sexual understanding," I toasted.

"Especially mine," she nodded, eyes glowing.

I reached for the telephone, but her hand was on mine, holding it still. "Not yet," she pleaded. "Make your call later. I want to talk first."

My shoulders shrugged. Walrus-moustache could wait a bit, I figured. Nobody was going to go barging into the Sheffield Inn. Most folks around these parts knew it was closed for the winter. So I sipped my martini and rested my elbows on the mahogany bar top.

"The first thing to talk about is getting yourself psyched for sex," I explained. "All our sexual hang-ups are usually the result of some traumatic experience of the past. In your case, it was a matter of listening too closely to what the good nuns taught you. A saintly life is not for everyone. Some of us aren't capable of living like saints.

"The human body makes certain demands on us. For some, those demands are damned difficult to ignore. For the saints, the demand isn't so great—it's all a matter of energy and health and hormones, anyhow—so they can pass up what the great majority of us humans really need."

Angela murmured, "My teaching has always been that to overcome those demands makes for a better person. To give in to them is a sin."

"Your church is changing its outlook. Today, if your conscience lets you do this or that without guilt feelings, it's fine. Or that's how I interpret the new doctrines. The world is getting more understanding about human—frailties, shall I say?—all the time."

Her tongue came out to lick her lips. Her dark eyes stared boldly at me above the rim of her cocktail glass as she drained it.

I reached to fill her up. Her large red mouth pursed, blew a kiss at me. The martini was getting to her, it was loosening the checkrein she had on her emotions. She was not drunk, but she was not so up-tight either.

"The trouble is, a lot of men and women in our western society have guilt feelings about sex. Thanks to the ascetic views of the early Christians, and to the grip these hysterical beliefs came to exert on the people of the western world, sex itself is considered to be a sin. You mustn't take pleasure in it, and if you have any fun while you're procreating the race, it's somehow wrong.

"A kind of hysterical misunderstanding put men like Simon Stylites on high pedestals, removing him and others like him from the world around them. Origenes castrated himself so he wouldn't be tempted. They were unreal, those men, in the sense that they retired from life while alive, in trying to purge their bodies of their human elements. Augustine, for instance, suggested that nobody should marry, so there would be no men and women in the future, and the end of the world would come so everyone could go to heaven.

"Poppycock! Sometimes I think our western civilization surrendered itself to madmen. But they've left their races on us all. Bluenoses and do-gooders have often banded together to repress everything that's any fun. They set themselves up as experts who know what is good for us, and what isn't. They tell us they know what we should look at and what we should read; and they so play on other peoples' guilt feelings that they get away with it. What gives them that right over the rest of us poor mortals?"

Angela nodded her head slowly, sipping the martini. "And you've found the answer to the problem?"

"I'd like to think so. Mine is a way of thinking, a positive approach to sex. Put away the traumas and psychoses, think naturally, let the body be itself. If the body wants to bed down, let it pick a friendly partner and go do it. It's good for the inner man. Coué was on the right track, except that he was concerned more with the well-being of the entire body than with its genital parts.

"With Coué, people of the Twenties psyched themselves to better health. With my book, they psyche themselves to a better sex life. No more guilt, no more hermits. Life is worth the living, so live it."

Angela Montosores put her drink down. Very seriously, she slid her right hand behind her back and ran the zipper of her dress down. She smiled at me as she shrugged her shoulders and tugged the bodice downward from her bosom.

"I want to do this," she said softly. "I want to be a woman, not just a mass of flesh and hair shaped in the female gender. I want to know what it is to cry out in pleasure, the pleasure I could never have with my own husband."

"What about the paella?"

"Oh, yes. The food. I'll cook dinner, but first—"

The bodice fell away from her black lace brassiere that was filled so admirably with her two generous breasts. I saw succulent breastflesh quiver to the movements of her hands and arms; the black cups could not quite contain those heavy globes. She glanced down at herself, she nodded her brown hair.

"I'm shameless," she said suddenly. "And I'm glad."

Her brown eyes lifted to stare at me. "I've always dreamed of doing something like this, of stripping myself in front of a man like any—no, I mustn't say the word *whore*—like an honest woman, rather. That is the way to think, isn't it?"

"You're making progress, Angela. I'm going to give you a copy of my book and let you browse through it while I go get that food out of the bags and ready for cooking."

I handed her a copy of my best seller. I caught her by the elbow and guided her across the thick carpeting to an easy chair. Her dress was still down about her middle. She drew away, put her hands to the dress, and shoved it down.

She was wearing a black girdle and gun-metal stockings above her high-heeled Pappagallos. And black panties. Her thighs were meaty but shapely, and the dusky flesh looked smooth and creamy above the stockingtops. She straightened proudly, looking me right in the eye.

"I'm psyching myself," she told me grimly. "Now let me read that damn book of yours."

She was almost half drunk. Another martini would have

turned her into a giggling goop. Right now she was pleasantly loose, happy to let down her hair, in the figurative sense, by taking off her dress. I thought it was a good first step. The rest could come a little later on.

So I left her with my book while I went into the kitchen and unpacked the various meats and arranged the spice cans from my spice rack, and laid out the carving knives with which to separate the bones and fat from the pork loins. I put the shallow paella pan on the stove but did not turn on the gas. Then I slid a scissors beside the knife with which to cut the shrimp into chunks.

I took my time, because we were in no hurry. The more she read, the more she would understand my philosophy and its attendant byways. I went back to the bar and mixed another martini. She was curled up in the easy chair, frowning slightly in concentration as she read on. At times she would turn back to study the many plates with which I had illustrated it.

Once or twice she flushed. Then she would bite her lip and psyche herself to read on. Her thighs were naked and appealing above her stockings, bisected as they were by the girdle garters. Her breasts seemed to be more solid than they had when she'd first slid down her dress. She was lost in a world of her own, but when she heard the spoon stirring my martini in the glass shaker, she looked up and smiled brightly at me.

"You really know how to get down inside a woman, Rod," she said thoughtfully. "You understand why it is that some women feel sex is dirty and disgusting. You know this is a wrong feeling, yet you don't condemn. You help by explaining that this attitude is wrong, that woman does herself more harm by maintaining it than she could ever do by letting herself do the things she unconsciously longs to do."

"Are you hinting?"

She laughed softly, saying, "Maybe I am."

"Then be my guest."

She drew a deep breath. Her breasts thrust up proudly in the black lace cups that held them. "I may just do that thing, Rod." Her eyes got a kind of glazed look.

I nodded, "You do that, Angela. I'll make my phone call."

My hand was interrupted as it reached for the telephone,

because the telephone began ringing. My hand continued on its journey, lifting the phone.

"Professor Damon here."

A very cultured voice said, "You are the Professor Damon who wrote *The Sex Machine?*" When I said I was he, the voice continued. "I am unofficial representative of Red China, Professor—calling you from Havana—to extend an invitation to visit our great country."

"Your country does me a great honor, but if you want me to lecture in Red China, let me remind you that your nation already has the greatest population in the world."

The voice chuckled. "It is not so much an invitation to lecture, Professor—as it is an invitation to perform, to prove your theories with a number of our loveliest Chinese girls.

"You see, our great leader, Mao Tse-tung, has already affirmed the fact that Chinese womanhood is more than capable of exhausting the love services of any man, no matter what his nationality, all in the service of the holy Mao. It is a sacred duty Chinese women owe the state, to please their men and fulfill their mutual function of reproducing many babies to praise Mao and grow up to take their places in our great country.

Yeah, hey. I answered, "It is a tremendous honor. I doubt very much if I'm worthy of it."

"Your personal safety is guaranteed, Professor. The only thing we cannot guarantee against is—your killing yourself in your vain attempts to prove that a capitalist can make love capably enough to satisfy our Chinese women."

There was a sneering challenge in the voice that made the hackles of my priapic pride stand up. No woman in the world can stay with my satyriasis. I have exhausted more than two dozen women of all nationalities at one bedding down, making them cry uncle to my phallic proddings.

"I have complete trust in my abilities, sir," I replied frostily. "This talent of mine has been proven beyond doubt. To make such a trip just to prove this sexual superiority of mine once more is out of the question."

"Think on it, Professor," said the voice. "I shall call back."

The line went dead. I shrugged, replaced the receiver, and glanced across the room at Angela Montosores. I damn near died. She was standing, swaying from side to side, her arms behind her back unfastening the strap of her black lace brassiere. She smiled at me the way a wanting woman has always smiled at a male.

My hands went on lifting the receiver and dialing Walrus-moustache. I ran my tongue around my lips as Angela pushed against a thin shoulderstrap. She smiled lazily at me and tugged the black lace downward. Her full white breast bounced a bit, freed of the constricting cup. Her brown areola was as big as a half dollar, and the nipple was rigidly thrusting forward.

I put the receiver to my ear. Walrus-moustache growled in it. "Must you always call me between the dessert and the brandy? What's on your mind?"

I told him about the two goons I had killed. He listened without a word. Then he sighed and muttered wearily, "Damon, I don't care about your little peccadilloes, as long as I don't have to clean up after you. Just because some blonde number wants to test your priapic powers—as advertised most thoroughly in your book, though inadvertently, I give you that much—there's no reason to go shooting people."

"They would have killed me," I snapped angrily. "Besides, the gun belonged to them, not to me."

"Oh, all right. I'll send a couple of Foundation agents over there to work with the police. I'll explain what happened to the district attorney. But the next time—"

"There's more, Chief."

I told him about the phone call from Havana.

"Ahhh," he breathed when I was done. "This does, indeed, become more interesting. You've foiled the Red Chinese on a number of occasions, Damon. This may be their way of getting even."

"By screwing me to death with their women?"

"Can you think of a better way to go?"

He had a point there. Still, since it was my life, I felt like arguing. I pointed out that my caller had admitted he could not guarantee my safety in the trials by which I was to demonstrate my sexual superiority over Chinese females.

As I talked, I looked up into the bar mirror that acts as a backing for the mahogany shelves that hold my liquor supplies. Angela Montosores was reflected in the mirror, staring down at her jutting breasts, her hands sliding upward under those protruding globes in a lifting movement. She let the breasts go as her palms brushed her thickened nipples and slid off.

Her breasts shook like dusky jelly, jiggling and quivering.

My manhood is a very sympathetic part of me. It responded to the sensual torture of those shaking breasts by swelling with pity. The swell became even more pronounced as Angela caught those protuberant nipples between her forefingers and thumbs and yanked on them. My boss-man was saying something but I don't know what. I was too mesmerized by those nipples. They must have been almost an inch long.

Angela was moaning, biting her lips as she stared down at her hands and her quivering breasts. Suddenly she looked up, saw me watching in the mirror. Her moist red mouth curved into a smile.

Determinedly, I turned away. I said into the telephone, "What do you want me to do?"

"Agree to go, nitwit! Do you realize what a golden opportunity you have to get a firsthand look inside the bamboo curtain? No Americans are ever allowed in there. But you're getting an invitation on a golden platter. Accept it!"

"Yeah, and gamble my life I'll get out with a whole skin."

"Professor Damon," said Walrus-moustache plaintively.

"Yeah, boss?"

"That's an order!" he yelled.

Two bare arms came around my middle. Inquisitive fingers stroked downward along my trousered thighs. The fingers paused, moved upward, gripped gently, then not so gently. My hips jerked in reflex, and I groaned.

"It isn't all that bad," said the boss-man. "I'm sure your hosts will take you on a couple of sight-seeing tours. Take along a Minox camera and take snapshots. We want to know if the Chinese are building any launching pads with which to hurl nuclear warheads at the Pacific Coast."

My zipper rasped. Warm fingers slipped into the opening it left. Then those fingers touched hot flesh. I groaned.

"Damon, will you stop making those uncouth noises? This is damned important. I was about to discipline you for having written that book. It was a damn fool thing to do, calling attention to yourself that way! But now, maybe it's not as bad as I thought."

Angela Montosores moved around in front of me, her eyes downcast at what her dusky hand was holding. Even as Walrus-moustache went on talking, telling me what an idiot I was to have held myself up to world opinion—and to possible reaction from some of the spy groups I had confounded in the past—Angela was slipping to her knees before me. Her eyes were glazed as they studied my phallus in its upstanding condition. She leaned forward and pressed her lips to me.

Then her tongue came out. While Walrus-moustache tongue-lashed me over the phone, this married woman tongue-lashed me in three dimensions. I was suffering above and below, though I must admit the suffering I was enduring below countertop was laced with pangs of exquisite pleasure.

After about ten minutes of explaining carefully just how many kinds of a buffoon I had been to write such a book and get it published, the boss-man grunted, "Well! That was my first reaction.

"But now, you've been given a heaven-sent—scratch that! —a hell-sent opportunity to go where no American has gone before in too long a time. Accept that invitation. Give it all you've got. Come back to me alive and well—and with plenty of snapshots. The Foundation will want to study them."

I was listening with half a heart. Most of my attention was on the rapture engraved on Angela Montosores' pretty face. She had psyched herself to a fare-thee-well, all right. Undoubtedly she had been fantasying some moment such as this in her daydreams or night dreams, but she had never before had the courage to drop to her knees before a man.

Her body was moving from side to side, I could see the faint movements of her girdled hips. She was in a catharsis of carnal contentment, purging herself of her fears and inhibitions. I did not disturb her. I was being the professor more than I was the man—at the moment.

Walrus-moustache muttered, "Keep me posted, Damon."

The line went dead. I was very much alive, in contrast. I hung up the receiver and reached down to clasp heavy breasts in my palms. Sliding my palms back and forth, I did what Angela herself had done—I lifted them up and let go of them so they shook and bounced. It seemed to give her some secret kind of kick because she made throaty noises and her lips opened wide to engulf me. I felt moist warmth and a gentle pressure.

I whispered, "Your poor knees must be hurt. Get up, honey. Let's get you comfortable."

She let me draw her from her self-imposed task. I studied her features carefully. She had no shame for what she had done, but a strange kind of pride, as if she finally realized her role as a woman.

"I'm glad I did," she muttered simply, smiling. "I've always wanted to do it. My—husband wanted me to do it, he wanted to do things like that to—to me. I told him it was disgusting, perverted. Now I realize I was the disgusting one. We could have been so happy if only I'd had the sense God gives little minks."

I said, "Is your husband still in town?"

She nodded. "Yes, of course, But I—"

Her face flushed, and her dark brown eyes were suddenly shy. "Do you think I could dare go to him and—and do what I did to you?"

"Tell me the answer to that later. Right now we're going to have ourselves a ball, you and I. Forget the paella. It's more important to your future that you frolic rather than feast."

She walked ahead of me into my bedroom, her thighs bare above the stockingtops and the lower edges of her buttocks bare below the black lastex girdle—she'd taken off her panties while I was on the phone—presenting me with a sexciting view. Mrs. Montosores would have no trouble with her mister, if her instincts worked the way they were working right now. I patted myself on the back, figuratively speaking. I was being the perfect professor, remolding a woman into what the good Lord had intended her to be.

Angela paused on the thick blue carpeting of my bedroom when I switched on the bed lamps on either side of the king-sized Empire bed with its blue and white counterpaine, with the inbuilt shelving behind the bed where there were books, and a supply of bottles and glasses and a small refrigerator that made ice cubes, a stereo set and various other items I might need when the spirit moved me. A writing desk and chair, an easy chair of navy blue leather, a number of oil paintings and framed lithographs occupied space on the floor and on the walls.

"It's beautiful," she breathed.

I patted her rump. "Off with the armor," I grinned.

Her fingers went to her girdle zipper. Then she was sliding out of it, unfastening her garterclasps, bending over with her flushed face set in mixed concentration and concupiscience, her dusky breasts dangling.

She made a mouth-watering sight, standing there all but naked. If her husband could have seen her right now, there would be no talk or separation or divorce but only of climbing between the sheets together.

I stepped behind her, kissed the nape of her neck. She gave a little gasp. My lips went down her soft back to the crease of her buttocks. I kissed her gently.

Foreplay is a most necessary part of the sexual union of man and woman. Too many men are apt to think only of their own bodily needs at a time like this. They ignore the equally erotic needs of their womenfolk. The more fools, they! If only they would read my book, they would understand that if they spent a little time readying the woman, their wives or their mistresses they would reap the benefits of their kisses and caresses.

People respond to emotion. And emotion is achieved by an appeal to their senses, of which we human beings have five. The main ones, where rumbusticating is involved, are sight, sound and smell. Taste and touch come in later. I was letting her see my aroused phallus, she was responding to the touch of my lips and tongue on her flesh, and to the strains of a rhythm band coming from the bed stereo, that switches on with the lights.

Conversation—hearing words as well as music—also plays a big part in precoital play. A woman likes to hear she is so damned attractive you just can't wait to drop her on a bed, even if she has no intention of going to bed with you. She likes to know and be told that she is desirable enough to be wanted.

So I kissed her back and buttocks, I paid her lingual compliments as well. "Your husband is an idiot. You are Venus and Aphrodite; your skin is cream flavored with musk. You could be Mrs. America, honey—and don't you ever forget it. Your legs are absolute perfection, and so's the rest of you. If you'd been there when Paris was judging the three godesses—which judgment led to the Trojan War—he'd have picked you any day of the week."

Pure slosh. But a woman eats it up. Especially if you mean it, which I did. Angela Montosores was a pussycat with perfect physical equipment. She gurgled to my adoration.

I straightened up, pressed against her soft rump. My arms went around her, my hands caught her breasts. I whispered into the pink ear half hidden under a spill of brown hair, "Finish undressing, then put your shoes back on. I'll show you a little trick to use on your husband when you go back to him."

She turned her head. "What makes you think I will?"

"You love him. You want to be a loving wife. This is an interlude, a kind of therapy. You know it and I know it. But you need it. You must get rid of your disgust, your inhibitions."

Angela nodded, eyes glowing. Giggling, she brushed her buttocks back and forth against me as if to show that she was willing to do what needed to be done.

In her high-heeled shoes she walked toward the bed, buttocks shaking loosely. I said, "Callimammapygian."

"How's that?" she asked, turning.

"Callimammapygian. It means you have a beautiful behind."

"Tell me more," she smiled.

"I'd rather show you."

It was my turn to kneel, to kiss her shapely legs, her slightly pouching belly and what lay in between. She crooned at me, she gasped and wept and sighed as I paid her femininity the tribute it should have known long ago. I explained the need for foreplay, the many ways in which a man and woman may please each other by caresses and kisses.

"Erotic arousal is a must before coitus, if the parties want to get the most from their relationship. Otherwise, it's usually all one-sided, as far as pleasure goes. But you act with him as you did with me, and I'm sure your husband will prove himself a perfect mate."

I pushed her gently back onto the edge of the bed. Her white thighs were slightly spread, but I widened them further and bestowed the Venus kiss on her flesh. Angela Montosores screamed in her delight. Her feet came up and then her high heels were acting like spurs on my back, goading me on in my worship.

"You learn fast." I said, grinning a little later as I drew back. "Those heels of yours were like spurs. Try that out on your husband."

Her hands were reaching for me as she wriggled back on the huge bed. They caught my shoulders, ran over them hungrily. She murmured, "Now, now, now."

I slid forward, making contact.

And then the bed telephone shrilled.

Without disturbing my partner I reached out a hand.

"Professor Damon? Your Red Chinese friend from Havanna calling. Have you given my offer any consideration at all?"

"I have, and the answer is yes." I murmured. "Though I should warn you, I am not going to fail."

"Excellent, Professor. And we know you must fail. It is the old story of the irrestible object meeting the immovable force. Let me warn you in return. There is an herb we have developed in accordance with our Maoist thinking, which we have named the Golden Lotus. It is an aphrodisiac of proven powers. It shall be fed to the girls you choose."

"You mean I get a selection?"

"Professor, we are not barbarians, despite what your government may think of us. China is a cultural nation, it is very ancient and filled with a reverence for knowledge that is almost an obsession.

"Furthermore, I pride myself on our politeness, and on our ability and will to pay handsomely for your endeavors. Shall we say a fee of one hundred thousand dollars?"

Beneath me, Angela Montosores was writhing and twisting, eyes closed and full lips slightly open. I got the notion she might be more comfortable, so I dragged a pillow from the headboard and pushed it under her buttocks. This elevated her pudendal region, and gave her hips freer play.

As she began sliding and bouncing, I said into the receiver, "If you are willing. I'd settle for something else."

"Ahh, and what is that, Professor?"

"A pillow book by Chou Fang."

"You know about our pillow books?"

"Oh, come now—er, by the way. What *is* your name?"

Ching Kow chuckled as he introduced himself. He added,

"And I must apologize. I just wasn't thinking when I asked if you knew about pillow books. I never stopped to think that an eroto-sociologist like yourself must indeed be familiar with these bridal boons to a happy sex life."

"One by Chou Fang. Or by T'ang Yin," I commented, ignoring the convulsing Angela Montosores under me. "I have some by the Ming period artists but none of the first two. And I feel that my collection for the League of Sexual Dynamics is sadly missing an important bit of erotic wisdom without them."

"You make me proud, Professor. I shall be happy to see what may be done. After all, one does more for someone who can appreciate the finer things of life. Oh, yes. And your fare will be paid by my county. I will arrange for transportation on a British Overseas Airways Corporation jet that leaves from Kennedy. I will be in touch. For now, farewell."

I hung up just as Angela was winding her soft, warm thighs about my middle, digging her heels into my behind as she jerked in sobbed enjoyment of the orgasmic pleasure which the French name *comble du bonheur* and the Japanese, *gokuraku-ojo*.

I can go on for hours without orgasm, because of my satyriasis. It's a mixed blessing, really. The women love it, but they sometimes think you're a bit inhuman. However, Angela Montosores was doing no thinking at the moment. She was bobbing her hips with machine-gun rapidity and emitting little mewling cries.

The telephone rang again.

It was Walrus-moustache, angry and indignant. "What cock and bull story did you dream up? There are no dead bodies at the Sheffield Inn! There were no bloodstains on its carpets. And there's no woman locked in any room."

I lay there stunned.

CHAPTER THREE

The boss-man was pulling my leg. He had to be!

"Oh, come on! I killed them, I locked the door on the woman, that Cassie. I saw the blood on the hall carpet, God-damnit!"

Fortunately Angela was off on cloud nine. She never heard a thing, because she was too deeply involved with what was happening to her body. Her hips kept flailing away at me, her thighs tightened around me, then loosened. Her brown hair, damp at her temples where she was sweating, was spread like a fan on the counterpane.

"Something's very wrong, professor," he muttered sourly.

I told him about my most recent phone call. I asked, "Do you think there's any possible connection?"

"Were the men who kidnapped you Chinese? Or the woman?"

"They were as American as Thanksgiving Day."

"Then Red China was not involved."

"Okay then. Who was? And why cover up what happened?"

"I'll let you discover the answer to that, professor. But only after you come back from Red China. The more I reflect on the opportunity you are being given, the more fascinated I am by it. Now, don't let me down."

"Have I ever?"

"There always has to be a first time," he commented darkly, and hung up.

Angela Montosores was orgasming this night for the first time in her life. She babbled about it. She had heard of this exquisite bliss, yet had never experienced it. Her case was not unusual, I told her, settling down into the rhythms of her moving hips. Many married women never experience the sexual orgasm all their lives, even women with children.

It seems incredible, but these are some of the facts of life as she is lived in the United States. Either their husbands and lovers ignore their bodily needs, or they have such deep traumas about the sex act that their minds will not allow their bodies to experience any pleasure. For both of these, I recommend my new book, *The Sex Machine.*

Much later, when we lay naked in the dim lamp light, her hand caressing my chest, she breathed, "You made me touch the stars, Rod. I'll always be grateful. Your book and your example have made me see myselff in an entirely different light."

I handed her the telephone. Her eyebrows shot up. "What's that for?"

"I thought you might want to call your husband. You are going to call him, aren't you?"

"Of course I am. In due time. Right now I intend to cook paella y sangria. You need food, lover. Then when we've eaten and sampled a few different drinks, I'm going to lead you by your—well, I'll lead you back to bed and you can show me some of the other things I've been missing all my life."

We fell asleep an hour past dawn.

Angela Montosores was going to open her husband's eyes pretty damn wide when she got around to making that telephone call. She was an avid learner, and she brought with her an eagerness to make up for lost and wasted time. We finished up a crash course in the space of one night.

After she left, I showered and dressed. I ate scrambled eggs and ham in my kitchen, waiting for a phone call from my communist friend in Havana. When the call still did not come, I got my Ventura Hangaway out of the closet and packed some go-away clothes.

Just as I locked the valise, my doorbell rang. I turned to my night table and opening the drawer, lifted out my blue-steel Luger automatic. I was in no mood for a rehash of last night's kidnapping caper.

I opened my apartment door to a well-dressed Chinese gentleman whose eyes beamed at sight of my weapon. He bowed politely as I invited him in.

"I'm not taking any chances," I told him.

"Very wise, Doctor Damon. Maoist China would approve your caution." His hand went into his coat pocket. "I have tickets for plane. And money for your use."

He passed over a leather billfold. There was a B.O.A.C. ticket inside that would take me to Hong Kong and back, plus the princely sum of five thousand American dollars in crisp new twenty dollar bills.

"For expenses," my visitor pointed out. "You will be met in Hong Kong, passed over border, escorted to Tin Song."

"Tin Song?"

He smiled toothily. "A village in interior where pretty girls are awaiting you. Very nice place, Tin Song. You will like it."

I promised him I would like it very much. He bowed, I bowed, and then I ushered him out.

A taxi drove me to the university airport. A private plane flew me to Kennedy airport. A pretty English miss at the

B.O.A.C. counter informed me that the VC-10 jetliner would fly to Chicago and San Francisco from New York. Then it would head out over the Pacific Ocean to Wake Island, then on to Tokyo. We would stop overnight in Tokyo to give our bodies a chance to unwind after the long flight. Reservations had been made for us in the Tokyo Hilton. Next day, we would fly to Hong Kong.

I dined on bay scallops and two Old Charter bourbons at Kennedy, lingering over my lunch because for the next day or two I would be scrunched down in an airplane seat while flying over half the world. I savored the sounds of people laughing and talking, walking around or bellying up to the bar. This was my last look at Uncle Sam for some time to come.

There was a woman dining alone, wearing a blue gabardine suit, the jacket open to display a frilled shirtwaist. She was not unattractive but her black hair was pulled back in a severe hairdo, and knotted in a bun at the base of her neck. She had high cheekbones and a full mouth without any lipstick on it. I tabbed her for a schoolteacher and an old maid.

She kept glancing at her wristwatch and it dawned on me that she might be on the same flight as I. Once she caught me looking at her and stared back frostily and glanced away. Her skirt was longer than usual. It even covered her kneecaps. A dried-up virgin, I thought.

I did not see her again until I got in line at Gate 8. She flashed her tickets ahead of me. I saw that she was seated in 7-E. I was in 7-F, which was a window seat. The old maid was going to be my companion for a while, it seemed.

As I trailed her across the tarmac toward the boarding ladder, I heard a faint rustle, as of silk. The sound puzzled me, because gabardine does not rustle. Then I decided she must be wearing a silk or taffeta slip.

A stewardess in a dark blue uniform gave me a happy smile, saying, "Welcome aboard, sir." She was a redhead, and she boasted a mild Scots burr.

The old maid must have glanced at my tickets too, because she was waiting in the aisle for me. She said coldly, "I believe you have the window seat. It will be easier for you to sit down if I wait."

I slid past her, then heard the silken rustle as she stepped after me, to plop her girdled behind down into 7-E. The sound really did surprise me, because with her lack of make-up and her long dress. I had her tabbed for a dame who would wear a plain linen slip, not one made of silk or taffeta. Still, you never know.

She did not cross her legs so I could catch a glimpse of the slip. She pressed her knees together primly, and sat with her hands folded in her lap. No rings on her fingers. No bells on her toes, for that matter.

"My name is Damon," I told the side of her face. "Professor Rod Damon. I teach sociology at the university."

She still stared straight ahead; rather rudely, I thought. Then she gave a little sigh and murmured, "I am Priscilla Saunders. Mrs. Priscilla Saunders." She saw my start of surprise, because she held her hands out before her. "You don't see a wedding ring. I—I have it in my bag."

Her hands flew to her handbag clasp. Next moment she was showing me a plain gold band. There was a slight flush in her face as she lifted her eyes toward me. "My husband is a missionary in Red China. I'm—on my way to join him, to—to get him out, if I may."

"The Red Chinese won't let him go?"

"No. They claim he's a spy for the C.I.A. It's completely ridiculous. Gavin couldn't spy for the Harper Valley P.T.A.! It's of a line with the rest of the Communist propaganda."

She sounded bitter and irrational. She put the gold wedding band back inside her plain leather handbag. "I don't wear it when I'm not—when he isn't here, while he's still in jail. It wouldn't be right. I'm not his wife right now, am I, with him a prisoner?"

"Well. . . ."

"I mean in actuality, not just in name."

This one was a kook. "Not really, I guess," I said.

She settled her head against the chairback and closed her eyes. The stewardess came down the aisle to take up a postion before the door into the big cockpit. She began her lecture about fastening our seatbelts and not smoking until we were in the air, all that jazz.

Priscilla Saunders paid strict attention, did everything she was told to do. Her face was very white, and it dawned on me that she might be scared witless.

I said soothingly, "It isn't so bad. The only sensation you'll feel is when the jet is racing for take-off speed, when the acceleration will push you back into your chair. Other than that, it's a piece of fudge."

She flashed me a grateful glance, though her smile seemed strained. "I've never been anywhere," she murmured. "I'm just an old stick-in-the-mud." Her cheeks reddened, and she looked down at her hands, which she was twisting together. "I don't know how I ever got the nerve to—do what I've done. But I'm going to see it through."

"Good girl," I said.

It was a change, talking to an old maid type who claimed to be married. Ususally I deal with women who are real dolls, honest swingers, members of the beautiful people. This one was a breath out of the middle west, corn-fed and pure as the falling snow.

The only thing that bugged me, was that silken rustle. She was not wearing a silk slip, nor even a taffeta one. It would call attention to her sex and Priscilla Saunders did not want anything like that to happen. She wanted to be a sexless nonentity.

I waited, I had plenty of time. She was on her way to Hong Kong, too, since that city is the entry port to Red China.

The VC-10 had made its run across the tarmac and was turning for its takeoff. I told the woman to close her eyes and lean back, to let herself go soft, not to be so tense. The big jet rumbled forward, faster and faster. Priscilla Saunders gave a little yelp, then she was utterly still. Her face was white, and her lips seemed to turn blue.

Then we were airborne and she opened her eyes wide in surprise and pleasure. She gave me a grateful smile. "It really wasn't so bad, it really wasn't. And thank you for all the help you've been. I do appreciate it."

Flying in a big VC-10 can be boring as hell. I was bored. I dozed and read. I ate the food the stewardesses brought me. I got out of the plane at San Francisco and bought a stack of paperbacks, then had me a few martinis. I got back in the plane and settled myself for some light reading.

Priscilla Saunders came running across the field. She was late. She held her hat with her left hand, her right arm clutching her plain leather handbag. I stared at her, thinking how much like an old maid she seemed, even with her wedding ring in her purse. I remembered her silken rustle too.

As she slid between the seats, her skirt got caught on the rack that holds magazines and reading materials. The hem pulled up to the middle of her surprisingly shapely stockinged thighs. I saw a garterclasp and pallid white thighmeat above it.

I saw no slip, not even a hint of one.

Now I *was* intrigued, because I heard the rustle as she pulled her skirt down. I guess she knew I'd seen her legs, she'd really given me quite an eyeful, because her cheeks went red and she sank down into her seat with a little cry of dismay.

"I'm sorry," she whispered, blushing all the more, "but I just couldn't help it. My skirt caught."

I chuckled. "A micro-skirt shows ever so much more, and you can see those on any city street in America or England." I leaned closer, whispering, "Your husband is a very lucky man."

She stared at me with eyes in which there was surprise, but no anger. As I say, a woman who is complimented on her attractiveness never gets angry at her flatterer, if it is done discreetly.

Still, she seemed to go back inside her shell, all the way across the Pacific, to Wake Island and then Tokyo. We were scheduled to stop overnight in Japan, so I offered to show Priscilla Saunders the the sights.

"They don't have a Yoshiwara district any more," I informed her, "but there is the Ginza and you might enjoy visiting it."

"No, thank you. I—I have a headache."

The eternal feminine plaint. I shrugged, made my apologies, and left her standing there in the aisle with her mouth open. Maybe I should have argued a little.

We were staying at the Tokyo Hilton, a lush hotel complex as modern as tomorrow morning. After a shower and a little nap, I moved down into the lobby, trying to make up my mind whether to eat in the hotel room and then hit the sack for a long sleep in bed, or go out on the town.

Priscilla Saunders decided things for me. I saw her glancing around the lobby furtively as she came out of the elevator and angled her sensible Enna Jettick shoes toward one of the side doors. Well, now! This was interesting. What was the prim Priscilla doing, acting like a secret agent? I decided the answer might prove fascinating.

I followed her along the sidewalk, half expecting her to call a taxi. She was having none of it. My interest in Priscilla Saunders increased when I saw two Chinese gentlemen following her. My hand went into my open jacket, loosing the Luger in my shoulder holster.

Why in hell should two Chinamen follow her?

I had to learn the answer, so I kept trailing her into a rather dilapidated section of the city. Tokyo has its slums, like any other city, though theirs seemed clearer than most. Tokyo itself is a very clean city, despite its ten million people. In the distance I could see the red haze caused by the bright neon lights of the Ginza section.

Apparently the meager dwellings and the narrow streets finally got through to her, because she started glancing around nervously. The two Chinese men hastened their steps. I started moving faster myself.

Where the shadows were dense and dark, they caught up to her. One man grabbed her with a hand spread across her mouth, his forefinger and thumb pinching her nostrils. The second man caught her arms and bent one up behind her back. Then the first guy put a hand under her skirt.

A rape!

But it made no sense. In Tokyo there are all kinds of places to go for sex. Bordellos, masseuse parlors, dance halls where you can select a partner not only for dancing but for later-on diddling. To rape a woman on the street, and most especially a foreign woman, made no sense.

Not only that, Priscilla Saunders wasn't all that sexy. She was about as exciting as a wet mop. However, there are no accounting for tastes. If these Chinese found her so irresistible, that was their business.

And mine.

I stepped forward and drove the edge of my hand in a karate blow to the back of a yellow neck. The man grunted and slid forward, releasing his hold on the lady's arms. His companion whirled, his left foot came up in a savage kick, aimed for my solar plexus.

There is a defense against such a kick. It is to grab that leg and swing it hard to one side. Naturally the kicker is on one foot. As his leg swings to one side, the foot on the ground slips and he loses his balance. The hands of the defender must be faster than the kicking foot to accomplish the defense properly.

My hands fastened on his ankle and yanked. He went flying sideways, upside down. His head cracked into a fire hydrant with enough force to kill him. He lay there like a lump as I turned toward Priscilla Saunders.

"You all right?"

She could not speak. Her mouth was open and her eyes bulged, but all she could do was nod her head up and down. I caught her elbow, lead her down the street and away from the unconscious men.

"Want to tell me what that was all about?" I asked.

She shook her head.

"Why'd they pick you to rape?"

"They weren't—"

She bit down on her lip. So! Rape was not the reason. But what was? What other reason would anyone have for molesting her? She did not seem like a rich girl.

"You got a lot of money in your bag?" I asked.

"N-no, of course not! It cost me almost all of my savings to make this trip."

We walked on. All around us the sounds and sights of Tokyo began to take shape. Tokyo is one of the largest cities in the world, if not actually the largest. There is a mingling here of East with West. Tokyo has its subway system, and many of its young men and women affect the styles of western dress. While it is true that the Yoshiwara district is no more, there is the Ginza, that is an entertainment wonderland in itself.

We were on the outskirts of the Ginza, which reaches from Kyovashi Bridge to the Shimbashi Bridge. It is a street to rival Broadway with its lights and color. It is a row of shops, of theatres, of any number of entertainment palaces.

My hand on her arm to guide her, I could feel that Priscilla Saunders was trembling in reaction to her experience. I decided she needed a bout of recreation to go with her scare.

"Do you dance?" I wondered out loud.

She gave me a quick glance, half suspicious, half thankful. "Why, yes, I do. Although I haven't danced for a very long time. Martin—that's my husband—doesn't exactly approve of dancing."

"Well, I don't want to—"

"No, no," she exclaimed. "I think under the circumstances, Martin might approve. Is isn't Sunday, you know—he's very much set against any form of fun on Sundays—and we've just been through a very terrifying experience. At least, it was terrifying to me. And so. . . ."

She let her words trail off, embarrassed. I could take the hint. Priscilla Saunders would dearly love to dance. She had been held down so long by her puritanical husband that any form of social camaraderie looked real good to her.

There were coffee shops and bars scattered here and there in this Yurakucho section of the Ginza. I figured a coffeeshop would be a little easier on her puritanism than a bar, where girls sometimes do a combination strip-tease and frug inside a birdcage affair suspended on chains.

I guess I was out of touch with my Tokyo coffeeshops, because no sooner were we in the door than a pretty Japanese hostess hip-wagged her way toward us, giving us both a toothy, friendly smile. Her black hair was done up with rhinestoned combs that gave a sparkle to the tier on tier of hair she had arranged in geisha girl fashion. She wore western shoes with high heels. In between the combs and the shoes was a black nylon dress that reached from her throat to her toes. The only thing was, the nylon dress was all she was wearing, and the nylon was transparent.

Priscilla Saunders gave a little gasp, then a rueful laugh. "I have been a stranger in the world, it seems. My goodness!"

I figured she would turn on an indignant heel and walk out of the establishment. Instead she gave me a big smile and nodded her head. "I would never dare tell Martin this, but I'm having a good time. And if you ever meet him, don't you tell on me."

I vowed silence as we followed the chubby buttocks of the hostess to a small table. I slipped a tip of a thousand yen into her palm. Instantly she was all attention. Her hand signaled a waitress as she bent to beam on my companion.

"Coffee?" she breathed.

I nodded. "Two, please. And a sweetbun or two if you have them."

Japanese coffee is a lot stronger than our American brand. It is slow-dripped and made of a carefully selected blend. The cream and sugar are mixed slowly, so that you get a drink that is almost a hot liqueur as the finished product. An American visitor tends to choke and gurgle after the first couple of mouthfuls, the way Priscilla Saunders did, but then the coffee really goes to work inside you and perks you up the way a drink or two can.

It perked my companion up, putting a faintly lopsided grin on her mouth and a spark in her black eyes. She nodded when I asked if she was enjoying herself. I noted that she kept staring at the waitresses who wore mini-skirted versions of the black nylon gown sported by the hostess. Her eyes kept getting biger and prettier, the more she looked.

It began to dawn on me that I might be able to discover what she was wearing under her severe dress that rustled like silk. I hadn't the fainest intention of this when I stepped into the coffeeshop, but her reaction to the semi-nudity of the waitresses lit the bonfire.

"Are you positive you don't know why those men accosted you?" I pressed, leaning forward and putting my hand over hers. Her flesh was quite warm. Well, maybe her blood was getting hotter.

"No," she murmured, staring at the tablecloth. She did not pull away her hand.

I said, "All right, we'll forget it then and chalk it up to experience. Where were you going when they stopped you?"

Her black eyes lifted, silently pleading with me not to go on questioning her. I think in another moment, she might have been crying. So I came up with a suggestion she really liked.

"Why don't we try dancing?"

She was out of her seat before I could push back my chair. There was a small open space in the middle of the tables that could be used for dancing, and it seemed like it was being used with a couple per square inch. They crowded you in like this on the Tokyo and New York subways during rush hours. Men and women were plastered belly to belly and buttocks to behind, moving lazily to the rhythm of a dreamy waltz.

I came up against Priscilla Saunders gently. I didn't want her to get ideas about me. The crowd took care of that part of it, however. Somebody rammed me from the back just as another couple nudged into her. We came together from knees to bosom. I could feel every square inch of her body plastered to mine.

She had few undergarments on under her plain dress. A brassiere and a pair of panties was my guess, and a garter-belt because she was wearing stockings. Other than that, she was naked under her frock. I heard a muffled gasp even as I was aware that her soft belly and rather large breasts were moving against me.

"Sorry about this," I murmured to her heavy black hair, since she was some inches shorter than the old professor. "If you'd rather sit it out?"

"No," she whispered. "I haven't danced in so long. . . ." She had a habit of letting her words trail off. We were shoved together like a mustard plaster on human flesh. Her thighs worked as she made dance steps, in such a way that they were inadvertently caressing me where I did my thing. My manhood is too responsive to such stimulation for me to ignore that subtle stroking. I enlarged.

Priscilla Saunders felt my male excitement. I held my breath, waiting for some sort of explosion. To my surprise, she put her head on my upper chest and squeezed even closer. My hand ran up and down her back. I heard the silken rustle again. She was too preoccupied by my arousal to pay any attention to what my hand did. Within limits, that is.

So I searched out her garments and her fleshy back with gentle fingertips. A brassiere-strap, a narrow affair that suggested something naughty in the way of a bra, and then, between the bra-strap and her panty, I came upon another garment. It was halfway down her back, it rustled, and it was not a slip.

I puzzled over the mystery of this silken what-not. It hung like a window shade behind her. It did not go all the way around her body.

My palm went down her back to her curving hip. Under my hand I felt warm flesh and the silken object. I drew a deep breath. I had to see how far down the thing went. I already knew that it was stitched to the back of her dress. My hand slid out onto a soft buttock.

She figured I was getting intimate; I honestly believe she hadn't the fainest idea of what I was up to; she gave another gasp and rammed her pelvis into me. Her thighs were slightly parted at the moment, in a dance-step. Then she felt a big part of me wedged between her inner thighs so that when she closed them, she had a grip on me.

Priscilla began to shake. She stumbled. A part of her was compelling her to keep that tight hold of me, but when she danced, she had to separate her thighs. She gave up dancing, just clung to me. It was easy on that postage-stamp dance floor, with all the men and women on it. Half of them were rubbing together the way we were, anyhow.

My hand slid across her buttock. She shivered. I ran a finger up and down her buttock crease and heard her moan. I honestly don't believe anybody had ever been this intimate with her body before, despite the fact that she was a married woman. And she loved it, in a dreamy, unreal way.

The silken thing went down below her soft buttocks. I couldn't follow it down any more without crouching, my hand was at the extreme limit. So I brought it up under her behind slowly, gently, half lifting her until she was feeling my priapic pride jammed against her mons veneris, and my fingers sunk into her buttocks.

We went on dancing. That is, we stayed in one spot and we moved back and forth. Being the founder of the League for Sexual Dynamics, I realized that my phallus was nudging her rigid clitoris, and that the clitoris, being the seat of all female sexual sensation, was reacting vigorously to that caress.

Her left arm was tight around my neck, helping her maintain her position. She gave a soft wail and then her hips began to slam back and forth as much as they could. She kept it up for minutes. I was praying the music would not stop. Then she whimpered and sagged against me so that it took all my strength to keep her upright.

Priscilla Saunders had orgasmed against my phallus. Within her, she was undergoing a climactic series of strange new sensations. I doubted seriously whether she had ever enjoyed an orgasm before. As the fierce delight of her climax ebbed away, as she regained her senses, so to speak, I had misgivings about her reaction.

I had no need to worry. When the music stopped, she lifted her flushed face to give me a long, bold look. Then her eyes fell, her hand hunted for mine, and she led the way out of the press of sweating bodies to our table. I signaled our waitress for refills with my free hand.

"What must you think of me?" she exclaimed under her breath.

"I think you'd better forgive me, first of all," I told her, clasping her hand. "It was the press of the crowd, plus the fact that you're a very attractive woman, that made me lose my head."

I took the blame. Hell, I had to remain friends with her until I learned what that silk thing was; I didn't want her to get mad at me. Telling her that her female charms caused my little slip in dance etiquette meant I was taking the blame for what had happened. Her conscience could let her off the hook. I caught the glimpse of her gratitude in her bright eyes before she lowered them.

"It—wasn't your fault," she said valiantly. "It was just —just the dance conditions. Yes, that was it."

She sounded as if she were justifying her erotic enjoyment to her husband. It would not be a sin if it happened because of external conditions; certainly she had not intended to get a deep sexual thrill when she got up to dance. I cursed the puritanism of our western civilization that could do this to a woman who had so much passion to offer a man. I wondered what her husband was like.

"Now forget it," I told her, seeing the waitress approaching. "We're going to have a good time and we aren't going to let one incident spoil the evening for us."

She gave a little laugh, nodding her head.

We sipped the coffee and we talked about world affairs. She was surprisingly knowledgeable about the Mideast crisis and other cold war incidents. She explained away my admiration by admitting that as a minister's wife—with her husband in Red China—she had very little to do but read newspapers and periodicals like *Time* and *Newsweek*. A corner of my mind told me she was a smouldering volcano ready to erupt under the right guidance.

I would have loved to serve as that guide, but my interest in Priscilla Saunders extended only to what she had sewn to her dress. The thought touched my mind that maybe I was the naive one. She might be a clever spy carrying secret documents to the Mao mob. Maybe there was no husband, maybe she had fed me a pack of clever lies.

Did I owe it to Walrus-moustache to find out? Or to the Thaddeux X. Coxe Foundation? I was not on any specific assignment, but I was an American and if there was any chicanery going on between Red China and a group of American dissidents, I really ought to find out about it.

I decided I had to get her dress off and examine it.

"Shall we dance again?" I asked gently.

She blushed scarlet, and shook her head.

"But I can't just take you back to the Hilton. We've been cooped up in the plane for such a long time, we both need some excitement. Yes, you too." I argued as she tried to slide her hand out from under mine. "You're going to be a long time in Red China."

I let her think about that as I waved the waitress over for more coffee. We had been nibbling on a sweetcake resembling a tart, made with plump, fresh Shizuoka strawberries.

Over our third cups, I suggested we visit a Turkish bath. It would give me an opportunity to get her dress off and examine it, I figured. She was warm and probably sweaty after what had happened; she went for the idea in a big way. Now there are Turkish baths and Turkish baths in Tokyo. I had one in mind that a fellow Coxeman had told me about, called Abiko's. You could take a lady friend there and undress with her in the same cubicle and employ two masseuses to work you over—and even more—on adjoining tables in full view of one another.

Outside on the sidewalk, I hailed a taxi.

The word Abiko was scrawled in red neon lights on a sign hanging before a doorway in what used to be the Yoshiwara district. I helped Priscilla Saunders from the taxi, paid the driver, and escorted her through the entrance into a lobby where a crystal fountain gurgled splashing waters over a miniature countryside done in terra-cotta and marble. Underfoot was a thick blue carpet, and ferns and garlands of flowers decorated the walls.

A young man was seated at a desk set cater-corner in the room. He looked up, smiled and nodded as I said, "My wife and I would like a Turkish bath."

I heard Priscilla make a protesting little sound. Maybe she had some idea of what was going to happen because she caught my arm and tugged it.

"I—I've changed my mind, d-dear. I think I'll settle for a shower in the hotel room."

"Oh, come on," I protested as a real husband might. "You

said when we agreed to make this trip that you'd go in for some fun and games. We lead a humdrum enough life as it is, back home in Indiana."

Her eyelids flickered. She was getting the message, all right, but I had to do it this way; I didn't want her thinking about the silk object I wanted to look at. Let her think I was ape for her body, it would keep her mind off my real objective. Her puritan training, her years as an obedient wife, warred with her natural inclinations.

The puritanism won. "I'm sorry," she whispered, staring at the carpeting, "but I—I can't."

She turned on a heel and walked out. I looked at the sympathetic clerk, shrugged, and went after her. Chalk one up for the opposition.

On the sidewalk, I caught up to her, where she was standing with her head bent, quietly crying. I put an arm about her shoulder, giving her a hug.

"Forget it," I said gruffly. "It was a stupid thing to do. I'm sorry. I should have known you wouln't go for it. On the dance floor. . . ."

I hugged her again. "Forget it. Back to the Hilton."

In the taxi, she was very quiet. She stared straight ahead, thoughtfully, and from time to time she sighed. If I am any judge of female sighs, she was regretting the lost opportunity to live a little. I began to hope. Maybe I could still get her dress off.

"I'm hungry," I said suddenly. "If you've really forgiven me, you'll let me buy you a nightcap and maybe some Welsh rarebit at the hotel grille."

She gave me a tiny smile, but shook her head.

We walked together across the lobby and went up to her room in the elevator. She was on the same floor as I was, three doors away. I took her room key from her fingers and unlocked the door.

She turned to take back the key as the door opened, but my hand at the small of her back urged her into the darkness. My hand hunted for a light switch, then the little bedroom was bathed in a pinkish light. With the other hand I closed the door behind us.

Her black eyes blinked at the light, then she said firmly, "Please. You must go. If anyone knew you were in here, my husband would surely hear about it."

I started to hand her the key, when my instincts told me she wanted me to make the play, so that she would have nothing with which to reproach herself. I had set the tone in the coffeeshop, by saying it had been the circumstances that were to blame for the ecstatic enjoyment of our dancing, not she herself.

Priscilla Saunders was a hypocrite, who wanted the fun without the self-incrimination. If I walked out of her hotel room now, after meekly handing over her room key, she would have nothing but contempt for me. And I could not blame her. She wanted me to throw her down on the bed that looked so inviting with its covers thrown back, but I had to make the play so she could accuse me of what happened—not to the world, but to her own conscience.

It dawned on me that she was a prime candidate for my book, *The Sex Machine,* just as Angela Montosores had been. I was not so much interested in making love to her, however, as I was in seeing what she had sewn to the inside of her dress.

I stepped forward, and my arms went about her middle.

My arms dragged her soft body up against mine. She cried out softly, and put her palms to my shoulders as if to push me away. There was no strength in her arms. She didn't want to discourage me too thoroughly; she was just putting up enough of a protest so she could tell herself later that I'd made her give in. Down there where our loins touched, she was hotly alive. She felt the phallic growth of my flesh, and her mons veneris came to meet it, remembering our dance.

"No," she whispered. "No, please."

Her voice was sultry. It was not denying me her body, it was just telling me the blame was on my head. Her face was flushed, her black hair had tumbled down a little so that she seemed far more attractive than she had at any time tonight. Her red mouth was a little open, and her lips were full and desirable.

I put my open lips to hers, felt her mouth give loosely to my kiss. She made tiny noises in her throat as she felt how aroused I was, and how suddenly. Priscilla Saunders knew nothing of my priapism that keeps me everready for a female frolic. She thought it was only because I found her intensely beddable.

My tongue went into her mouth, found her own moist tongue and caressed it. She began to whimper; her arms came up around my neck in a regular stranglehold. She began bumping her soft hips at me.

I caught the zipper of that damn dress and ran it down. She tried to pull back from me but my hot palms were on the nakedness of her back between her brassiere and her panties, and they were more than she could fight. Her belly began to squirm lazily back and forth against me, as her thighs sought to widen and catch me prisoner once more.

My fingers caught the shoulders of her dress, slid it down her arms. She quivered, waiting, suspended between the realism and the fantasy of her sensual needs. The dress dropped to the upper swells of her breasts, then slid off them. In the black net brassiere she affected, her breasts were big and firm. Their light brown nipples were stiffly erected against large, dark areolas.

I pushed the dress to her middle and then down over her wide hips. She stepped back obligingly as she let me see her black garterbelt and—marvel of marvels!—a pair of black lace bikini panties.

I grinned at her. "Martin must be quite a boy if he likes you to dress in underwear like that!"

She blushed all over. "He doesn't—know about it. He's never seen me in my underwear."

I almost forgot about the dress, as it fell to her feet. Her thighs were plumply white above her black nylons. She looked like a color fold-out page of a man's magazine. The net brassiere was as transparent as the gown the hostess had worn in the coffee shop. So were the bikini panties, that showed off a fluffy mass of hair.

She was really something without that dress. Her body was soft and curved. She was a real woman despite her puritanistic tendencies. And despite the fact that she was still blushing, she enjoyed my appreciative stare. She had been so long without a man that she was damn near dying.

I looked down at the dress crumpled on the carpet, I knelt down, told her to lift her legs. I was up close to her, I caught a whiff of perfume and that female scent that told me she was in heat. One after the other she raised those shapely gams and let me draw the dress out from under her.

I pretended to be surprised when I saw the long pieces of silk stitched to the inside of her dress. "Oh? What's this?"

She made a grab for the silk, crying out. I held her off with an arm, kneeling there before her, smiling up at her.

"Come on, tell me," I urged playfully.

"No! I can't! Please, it's very important."

She came closer so that the warm flesh of her thighs was against my face as she strove to snatch away her dress. I pretended to be off-balance. I let her thighs push me to the floor, so that she was sprawled over me with the vee of her legs at right my mouth.

I opened my mouth and bit gently into that flesh-fork.

Nobody had ever been that intimate with her. She screeched and scrambled free of me on hands and knees. She sat on the floor, her legs drawn up under her, and stared at my face with horrified eyes. Priscilla Saunders made a most attractive picture, but I was going to find out what that silken thing was if it killed me.

I tugged at the threads, snapped them gently so as not to harm the silk itself. To my surprise, I heard her crying softly.

She had buried her face in her hands, and was weeping a flood. I said uncomfortably, "Oh, stop it. I'm not going to turn you in."

She lowered her hands, gaping at me in amazement. "Turn me in?"

"For a spy." I shook the dress at her. "That's what this this thing is, isn't it? Some sort of coded message to the Chinese Reds? You're no more a missionary's wife than I am. You're a secret agent, honey."

She began to laugh hysterically. I am sure she had never spent a night like this in her life, and it was bound to make her let go of her rigid controls. She laughed and laughed, half sobbing all the time. I began to be afraid she might get really hysterical on me, so I reached out and grabbed her by the long black hair that was half down her bare shoulders.

I shook her head back and forth until she yelped at me angrily. Anger was better than hysteria. I let her go.

"Keep quiet," I growled. "If you aren't a spy, what are you?"

"A missionary's wife," she snapped.

"And what's this?" I snapped back.

"You wouldn't know," she sneered.

So I looked. I got the threads undone and very carefully lifted the length of silk which, as I untangled it, became half a dozen silken scrolls. I spread them out and stared at them disbelievingly.

"My God!" I whispered. "Do you know what you have here?"

I would have given an arm and a leg for those scrolls to be mine.

CHAPTER FOUR

She nodded quietly.

"Yes, I know. They belonged to my husband's father."

"These things, these six scrolls are absolutely priceless! They're the work of Chao Meng Fu, who painted in the last quarter of the thirteenth and first quarter of the fourteenth centuries, during the Yuan dynasty!

"These pictures are almost legendary. They show the six postures of the fifth century goddess-queen of the west, Hsi Wang Mu. She took young boys as her lovers so that their Yang essence could give her eternal youthfulness. I've read about these six scrolls—but I never believed they existed.

"It's like finding half a dozen authenticated paintings by Raphael or Michelangelo, buried away in an attic. It's a miracle."

I was honestly overcome. A collector, if he had the money, might pay half a billion dollars for these scrolls. Or even more. They were without price, being so perfect and so unique. I stared down at them, then raised my eyes to Priscilla Saunders.

"You're no spy," I amended. "You're a crook."

She shook her head, making her long brown hair loosen even more, giving her a wanton look. "No, I'm no crook. Those things really did belong to my father-in-law. They were given to him by my husband's grandfather, who served in the Boxer Rebellion as a United States Marine."

She told me the story in a low monotone, as if she was ashamed of it, not looking at me, but at her fingers that she interlaced together and wrung from time to time.

His name was Alfred Saunders. He had run away from the Indiana farm that was his home at the age of nineteen and joined the Marines. He had been in the Pacific theater when the Boxer Rebellion started, and had been ordered with his unit to Taku.

"I don't know how much you know about the Boxer rebellion," she went on. "It began in 1900 when a number of Chinese patriots calling themselves the Boxers, formed together from the peasant class to fight oppression, floods and famine. The dowager empress opposed them at first, but when the Boxers began slaughtering missionaries and their families, she decided to turn them against the foreigners, much as Mao Tse-tung unleashed his Red Guards a few years back against certain elements in his own society.

"The Europeans took refuge behind the walls of the Peking legation. They had little food but they fought bravely against the attacks of the Boxers aided by the Chinese Imperial troops. Naturally the other nations of the world could not let them be slaughtered. So England, Germany, the United States, France, all sent their crack troops into combat.

"Those troops landed at Taku, seized the forts and went by rail into the interior, attacked here and there by the Boxers. They weren't sure just how large a force they were to fight so they delayed getting on to Peking for almost a month.

"At the request of the Kaiser, the supreme commander of the allied forces was Count Alfred von Waldersee. Under his command, the allies besieged Peking, entered it and defeated the Boxers and the Imperial troops in a number of bloody battles.

"After the victory, the looting began."

She paused to draw breath, staring down at her feet. "There was plenty to be looted. Peking was an art treasure itself in those days, and it held treasures"—her hand gestured casually at the scrolls—"to make the mouth of a collector water.

"My husband's grandfather used to say that among the Allies, there were 'amateur' collectors and 'serious' collectors. He had saved the life of a mandarin who was angry at the dowager empress, Tz'u Hsi, for some real or fancied insult. He showed my husband's grandfather where those scrolls were hidden."

Priscilla smiled faintly, brushing back her fallen hair with her fingertips. "I don't think grandfather realized what a treasure had been given him. To him, they were just dirty pictures. He stole a few other things—some bronzes, a couple of paintings of non-erotic variety—and with them in his warbag, came home to prosper as a feed and grain merchant.

"He sold the paintings and the bronzes, but he could never quite dare to part with the scrolls. Personally, I believe he was ashamed of having taken them. People looked on things differently in those days."

I studied the scrolls, my heart still hammering out a fandango.

"As far as title goes, I suppose," I murmured, "since there's no more dowager empress—he has as good a right to them as anybody. But how did the Red Chinese know you had the scrolls?"

"My husband blabbed, offering them in return for his freedom. There was a wait, the Red Chinese had to consult one of the few scholars they've allowed to live. When he told the Party how priceless those scrolls are, the offer was made to my husband. I would be furnished with an airplane ticket to Hong Kong, together with some spending money—I guess they knew how poor we are—if I would bring the scrolls into Red China. Then they'd set my husband free."

I began rolling up the scrolls very carefully.

"What are you going to do now?" I asked.

She shrugged casually. "Go on to Hong Kong, take the scrolls to be studied. Then go into Red China."

She had lost interest in her libido, I was sorry to see. Even as she finished speaking she stared down at her fleshy body so flully displayed, flushed and reached for a robe. She slipped into it, standing before me. Her breasts bounced half out of her black brassiere as she wriggled her arms into the sleeves.

"You're a tease," I grinned.

She blushed even more. She said, "I—I'm tired, all of a sudden. You—you won't mind, will you, Rod?"

"Of course I mind," I told her. "But I'm no rapist. If you say no, then it'll be no. Though with infinite regrets on my part."

Her quivering hands tied the belt about her waist. Her

breasts were almost fully revealed in the low cut of her collar, but she was otherwise decent enough. I sighed for what might have been.

I got to my feet and held out the scrolls. "Sew these back onto your dress. It makes as good a hiding place as any." A thought struck me. "You sure you don't want me to sleep here? I mean on the couch, while you're in your bed? I wouldn't put it past the Red Chinese to make another try for the scrolls."

She shook her head. "No. I'll be fine, thank you."

My own room seemed barren and lonely when I got back to it. The first thing I did was bring my Lugar automatic out of the bag where I'd been keeping it, together with its shoulder holster. Next time I might not be so lucky, or the men after those scrolls might be armed. I decided not to take chances.

I waited next morning, until Priscilla Saunders came out of her room. Then I joined her for breakfast.

"I've put you under my protection," I informed her.

I heard the rustle of silk as we walked toward our breakfast table to feast on ham and eggs, buns and coffee. Our plane was taking off at noon, it was only a three-hour flight from Tokyo to Hong Kong. We chatted casually about world affairs. Priscilla confessed that she was still worried about her husband; he might be dead for all she knew. Her last letter from him had been more than six months ago; all the negotiations for the scrolls had been carried on by the Red Chinese.

I patted her hand and tried to cheer her. I was positive she was regretting her failure to let herself go with me in her bed. If her mind was not, certainly her female parts were. She was one needy woman.

We taxied to the airport and got back into our seats.

She was not so afraid now. She was becoming a veteran of the airways. Her eyes flashed proudly at me as she unfastened her seatbelt while we flew high above Kyushu island.

"You'll be a world traveler yet," I grinned.

"If I ever get out of China alive."

I told her not to worry, her trip into the interior—she was headed somewhere around Lingling—would be attended with a lot of publicity. She shook her head at that, told me that the Red Chinese had forbidden any publicity whatsoever. Nobody except me knew where she was headed, and why.

"Where are you staying in Hong Kong?" I asked.

"The Carlton."

"Too far out of town. I want you to be close at hand where I can keep an eye on you until you make that trip. We don't want you to get yourself killed before you even get inside Red China, now do we?"

She agreed to do what I advised. I asked the stewardness to radio on to Hong Kong and make reservations for Priscilla Saunders at the Hilton, where I had my room. Then we settled back to doze a little and sip the tea which the girls in blue were serving.

Hong Kong is a British Crown Colony. It has no musuems, no monuments of any interest, yet it is one of the most fascinating cities in the world. There is a large Chinese section, it has been said that any time it wants, Red China could take Hong Kong for its own. But it is so necessary to the economy of the huge country that it is considered quite safe from attack.

The stores teem in Hong Kong, and you can always buy at discount prices. Red China sends much of its wares to Hong Kong. Every year it grosses in the vicinity of close to half a billion dollars from its Hong Kong trade, a million a day in the food alone which it furnishes. So the eighteen-mile-wide corridor from Red China to Hong Kong is kept open. There are three million people living in the twelve square miles of habitable land that is Hong Kong proper. One third of these are Chinese, who maintain most of the outlet stores which display and sell wares and goods from their huge homeland.

Since the Korean War, Hong Kong has been slowly turning into an industrial city. Public housing projects have changed the old Shek Kip Mei shacks and huts into reasonably decent apartment compounds. Labor is cheap. So that today the city is not merely a trading post, it is actively engaged in competing with Lancashire cotton goods and American linen-ware, among other items.

The traveler rarely sees this part of Hong Kong. He is more interested in the vast shopping district that is Kowloon. Here among the ladder streets are stores where a man or woman can buy almost anything—cheap, by American standards. It is in these shops and along the clean white sands of Repulse Bay, where the finest swimming is, that the traveler is most often seen.

Priscilla Saunders admitted that she would dearly love to shop in the ladder streets. What woman wouldn't? But she had to go at once to the art galleries of Pak Dong to have her scrolls looked at. The sooner she was with her husband, the better.

We came down at Kai Tak airport without incident.

The Hong Kong Hilton is a big slice of western life decorated with Eastern touches. It had reserved a room for Priscilla Saunders and at my request it changed that room to move her across the hall from my own room. By this time it was late afternoon.

I suggested we go swimming at Repulse Bay, then dine together in the hotel. She pleaded tiredness and a desire to visit Pak Dong and have her scrolls verified as the work of Chao Meng Fu. She would shower, take a rest, then set out for the ladder streets of Kowloon.

My shoulders shrugged. So be it. I promised myself I would not be that eager to put myself in Red Chinese hands. So after a shower, I put on a lightweight business suit and my shoulder holster with the Luger fitting loosely into it, and knocked on her door.

She was ready, in a linen dress that came down below her knees. Her black hair was parted in the middle and drawn back in a bun at the base of her neck. She looked like my maiden Aunt Tillie.

"Why do you put yourself down all the time?" I said.

"I couldn't wear those mini-skirts the young girls adopt. I'd die of shame."

"I don't see why not. You have damn good legs. But you don't have to wear mini-skirts to look presentable."

She got angry at that, and maybe I didn't blame her. But it puzzled the hell out of me why a woman who was as handsome as Priscilla Saunders, and with the body she could flaunt, chose to make herself up like a character in a movie.

In the taxi to Kowloon, she sat as far from me as possible, staring straight ahead. It was all right with me; I wasn't romancing her. I was just playing bodyguard. We were silent along Queen's Road East and Queen's Road Central. We might have been lovers having a quarrel.

When we got out and while I was paying the taxi driver, telling him to wait for us and giving him a huge tip of twenty Hong Kong dollars—about three-fifty, American—to make sure he did, Priscilla set off by herself. We were in the shopping district, there were signs in Chinese hanging overhead while the smells of roast duck and frying pórk intruded on us everywhere. It was growing dusk, and the shadows were getting longer.

I frankly didn't go for the running-away act my companion was putting on. Already she was about fifty feet ahead of me. I was afraid I might lose her in the crowd. So I hurried my steps to a half run, and when she turned sideways into a ladder street and began going up the stairs, I wasn't too far behind her.

Maybe that distance between us was a lucky thing. Because I was able to see four young, husky Chinamen step out of the shadows at sight of the woman, and move after her. I slowed my pace but I put my hand inside my coat pocket to the Luger and loosed it in the holster.

They were on top of her in a blurring movement that bespoke long practice at the art of robbery. One of them clamped a hand over her mouth and an arm about her neck. A second grabbed her skirt hem and yanked it up to show off her handsome legs in gun-metal nylons and red-and-black lace panties, plus a garterbelt to match.

The goons were not intent on sex. They wanted those scrolls. The second man produced a sharp knife, bent forward and began to saw at the threading with which Mrs. Saunders had resewed the scrolls into her dress. The threads started falling away.

The fourth man was the lookout. He crouched in the shadows, staring around him. When he saw me coming up the steps three at a time he moved out of the shadows to stop me, waving an arm and yelling in Chinese at me.

"*Ni Hao!* You go 'way!"

I didn't waste any breath on him; I just kept on coming. He sprang to meet me, hands out and fingers widespread to grip and choke. He must have figured I was a dumb western tourist seeing a lady in distress. His contempt was written all over his face. He would choke me a little, knock me down and kick me a few times just to teach me to mind my own business.

My hand caught his wrist and whirled. I caught the impact of his lunge on my back as I bent. His body rose upward. I yanked hard on his arm. He went flying through the air.

His high-pitched yell of surprise stopped when he hit the brick wall of a building. He slammed into it hard and slid, still upside-down, to the street. He was out cold.

I paid him no more attention, too busy with the man who had been holding Priscilla Saunders. He leaped away from her and whipped out a knife, coming at me on the run.

I met him more than halfway, dodging a wicked slash of the sharp blade, pivoting on a heel and ramming my fist into his belly. He grunted and rocked back a foot. He was a dangerous man with that knife in his hand so I forgot about chivalry and brought my heel up, right into his manhood.

He screamed and dropped, clinging with both hands to his most precious possessions. The knife flew through the air to clank against the flaggings of the steps. His body flipflopped up and down as he went on screeching.

The man who was working on the scrolls never turned his head. He got them undone, he did not dare rip them so as to put a tear in the scrolls; he had been well-briefed as to their value. He let the third man come for me.

I could have shot them both, of course. But I wanted no more trouble, and the Hong Kong police might interfere at the sound of a shot. I dropped to one knee and my hands went out to grab him by his left ankle and knee.

He yelped in surprise. By that time I was putting pressure on the knee, pushing at it while I yanked his left foot toward me.

He went backward, off balance.

I dove for him, the Lugar in my hand. I slammed the barrel across his temple, hard. His eyes rolled in his head and he sagged limply as the body bounced. I recovered my balance and turned toward Priscilla Saunders.

Before he could come to me, the last man had to let her go. She was busy fighting for her scrolls, tearing scratches down the face of the burly young tough, who had managed to get the scrolls by this time, but who couldn't duck away from her fingers.

I was on top of them both in an instant.

My right foot came up in a savate kick. My heel thudded

into the side of his jaw. He whooshed and sagged. I leaped on him, slammed the Lugar barrel under his jaw. He lay like a dead man.

I eased the scrolls from his hands.

Priscilla Saunders was crying, now that it was over. "Wha—what would I have d-done without you?" she sobbed.

"You'd have been in a bad way, but never mind that. Where's Pak Dong's shop?"

"This—this way!"

We ducked under a big sign about a hundred yards from where the four goons lay. Priscilla opened the door. A bell sounded in the rear of a neat little shop covered from floor to ceiling with art objects thrown on tables, hung from wall pegs, dangling from the ceiling on lengths of string. Shelvings held statues and ceramics. Everything I saw was beautiful. Pak Dong was a connoisseur of Chinese art, all right.

He came from the rear, an old man with a wispy white beard and a bald pate, in black shantung mandarin coat. His black eyes were bright and sly. He made a little bow. From his first glimpse of us, his eyes had been drawn to the scrolls that I held in my fist.

"Ahh, welcome, American visitors. You wish to trade?"

Priscilla said, "I've b-brought the s-scrolls."

The thin white eyebrows lifted. "Scrolls?"

I told him, "The six scrolls of Chao Meng Fu. The legendary paintings about Hsi Wang Mu and her young lovers in their attitudes of love worship."

His eyes turned to me, surprise plain to read in them. "You know of Chao Meng Fu? Of the goddess-queen of the west?"

"I know these scrolls are priceless. I'd give an arm to own them. We're here to have you verify their authenticity. But you know all about that."

Pak Dong looked irriated. I am sure he knew of the attack to be made on us; he never expected to see the scrolls with Priscilla Saunders. But he made the best of a bad bargain.

He bowed low. "If this is true, please to enter my establishment. It will be an honor to see the work of Chao Meng Fu, if it is his work."

I figured I might as well let him know we were no babes in the woods. "It's his work, no doubt about it. I've seen enough Chinese erotic art to know. But don't take my word for it, have a look yourself."

He did not believe we possessed original art by the great master. In his place, I might not have believed it either. He was going on orders from Mao Tse-tung, I think, or from someone else who was high up in the Chinese hierarchy. He was to give his opinion, and arrange for further travel by Mrs. Saunders if, by some miracle of fate, these were authentic paintings.

He led the way into the rear of his gallery, which was a combination office and workshop. He extended a hand for the scrolls. I handed them to him.

Quite casually he unwrapped them and took a glance at the first one. His whole body stiffened, his mouth opened and the breath wheezed in his throat. He bent forward, forgetting our presence.

His bright black eyes scanned that first silken scroll, up and down and sideways. He was hunting for the telltale signs that would say, as might the voice of Chao Meng Fu from the grave, that this was his work.

"Ho t' sai," he breathed.

He placed the first painting very reverently on his desk. He examined the second scroll just as carefully. One by one, he went through them all. When he raised his head, I saw tears in his eyes.

"It is so. These are the works of Chao Meng Fu! I never believed I would see them. I did not believe they existed, though I have heard rumors that once they might be seen in the Imperial Palace in Peking. They have been gone from China for half a century."

"Now they are back," I murmured. "And they will be turned over to the Mao government, if the Reverend Martin Saunders is allowed to leave Red China."

The old head bobbed in agreement. "Of course, of course. It shall be done at once. You may stay to verify the fact."

He reached for a telephone. Moments later he was talking Chinese into the phone so fast I could hardly follow it. I am a good linguist and I have mastered several of the Chinese dialects, but this was a new one on me. I got a few words, no more, but the substance of the conversation was clear enough.

The American lady had the scrolls. Yes, yes, they are

the work of the fabled Chao Meng Fu. Art treasures worth all the money Red China could pay. It was a crime for them to be outside the motherland. China must have them back again at all costs.

He would arrange for the passage of the American lady, with his own funds he would buy her ticket into the provinces of Kwantung and Hunan. He would write out the papers with his own hand that would give her safe conduct.

He listened for a time; to words of praise, I imagine, for a job well done, because he beamed and nodded. When he hung up, he was very businesslike.

"I shall hold the scrolls here while——"

"Hold it, Pak Dong," I snapped. "None of your oriental tricks. The scrolls stay with the lady until her husband is released."

He looked disappointed, but shrugged philosophically. He sat down at his desk and scratched Chinese characters on a sheet of rice paper. This he handed to Priscilla Saunders. He scowled at me.

"Do you accompany the American lady?"

"Unfortunately, no."

He nodded thoughtfully. I was certain he was turning over possibilities of getting Priscilla alone and talking her out of the scrolls or taking them away from her by brute force. His wizened body could not apply that force, but four goons like the men I'd left on the street easily could.

I lifted out my Luger. I put the barrel under his nose. He stared at it in horror as I said, "In case an accident happens to her in Hong Kong, I'll come back here and blow your goddamned head off."

He glared at me in utter hatred, but he nodded. There are men who only understand force and brutality. Pak Dong was one of them.

We showed ourselves out.

As we walked toward the taxi, we saw a crowd about the four goons. There was a Hong Kong policeman, taking notes. We skirted the crowd; I respected Priscilla's wishes for no publicity, though I personally felt some publicity might help her once she got inside the Chinese border.

The taxi took us back to the hotel.

We dined together. Over the dessert and coffee, a man approached the table. He bowed low and handed an envelope to my companion. It contained papers that would see her safely into China and to a village named Hok Tang and back again to Hong Kong.

She would be met at six the following morning.

There went any ideas I might have had about picking up where we'd left off in her Tokyo hotel room. She had to be up early tomorrow morning, which meant she must get a good night's rest. I shrugged, kissed her good night and good-bye at her door.

I went into my own room and switched on the light. There was a girl in a blue silk dress sitting in the one easy chair. She opened her eyes at sight of me and smiled with full red lips.

CHAPTER FIVE

"Good evening," she caroled. "I am Ip Chung."

"I must recommend the Hong Kong Hilton to my many friends," I commented, making a little bow. "Are you my hostess for the night?"

"I am not from the hotel. I come from Mao Tse-tung. I have been sent to find out if you are the Professor Rod Damon the great leader is expecting to come to Tin Song."

"I am, I am. Believe me."

I was in no mood for any tests. I was too worried about Priscilla Saunders and her coming trip to Hok Tang. The girl smiled and shook her head.

She was a beautiful thing. Her skin was soft, smooth, and tinted a very faint gold. Her thick black hair was set very tastefully, curved above her high forehead and hanging down her throat to her shoulders and the small of her back. The dress fit her like a wet bathing suit, outlining rather full breasts for a Chinese, with nipples that made sharp dots in the jacket. Her thighs seemed plump, her legs shapely. Where the slit in the side opened, I got a look at those legs from her slippered feet almost to her buttocks.

I opened the door. "Good night," I said, smiling.

She shook her head, also smiling. "I am not permitted to leave without testing you, Professor. Please accept that fact."

Her English was flawless. She must have been educated

in an English school, perhaps a missionary school. She spoke with the faintest hint of an English accent, but from her it sounded good.

"All right," I surrendered. "Ask away."

I moved across the room to the dresser, yanking at my tie and beginning to unbutton my shirt. I took my coat off and hung it in the closet. I dropped the tie on the dresser top. Then I pulled my shirt-tails out, before turning to the girl.

She was standing, bending a little and gripping the hem of her dress with red-nailed fingers. The Chinese garment was coming up her legs, slowly and with deliberate laziness. She lifted her head, challenged me with her eyes.

"The test does not consist of questions, but of deeds," she breathed. "You have the reputation of being a great lover. I am here to test that ability. If you can tire me out, then I shall say you are the real Professor Rod Damon."

"Just like that, hey? Maybe I don't want to make love. Did your bosses ever think about that?"

"Then you are not the real Rod Damon!"

I did not feel like making love, at least not with this Chinese doll. With Priscilla Saunders—well, maybe. Not that I was any prima donna, you understand. I usually grab my loving where I can get it. I rarely turn down an invitation. But I did have Mrs. Saunders on my mind.

My spirit may have been willing to turn down Ip Chung, my body was something else again. She was holding her hem about her upper thighs and my manhood was telling me how much it enjoyed the sight of her shapely legs by swelling with excitement.

She saw the bulge, and laughed.

"You are the professor!" she cried. "I am glad. I have not wasted my time."

"That's settled, then," I nodded. "Now you can go."

"Oh, no!" She looked horrified. "I have not really tested you, as I have been instructed. You have just given me proof that you may be the man whose name you use. No more."

The skirt rose slightly.

I felt my mouth getting dry as my eyes took in the shaven mount with its deep pink dimple. Her mons veneris was high, plump. It was larger than the normal Chinese motte, which made me think this doll might have Causcasian blood in her.

She laughed softly, reading the expression on my face. I have a very low boiling point where a pretty women is concerned. My physical make-up, my priapism, is to blame for this. I forgot all about Priscilla Saunders. I'm afraid. This golden honey-pot, this Ip Chung, was really getting to me.

I lifted off my shirt and tossed it. My fingers went to my belt buckle, loosening it. I shoved down my neatly pressed trousers and let them lie where they pooled at my feet. I was down to my boxer shorts.

Her red mouth made a moue at sight of my manhood standing there and shoving out my shorts, making a tent. Upward went the dress above her deeply naveled bowl of belly. Just under her breasts it paused. She was sin incarnate.

"You first," she hinted.

I grinned. Down went my shorts, up went my phallus.

My feet carried me forward until my flesh was nudging her pudendal dimple. She was breathing faster, her eyelids dropped so that her eyes were mere slits. Her belly moved in and out, firming outward, then hollowing.

Very slowly, she began a rhythmic swinging of her naked hips. I felt something hard growing in that dimple and knew it for her clitoral bud. Ip Chung was stimulating herself with her movements, just as swiftly as she was stimulating me. Her heavy red lips were parted to aid her breathing.

I leaned forward, put my open lips to hers. She whimpered, mouth opening in turn to accept my darting tongue. I kissed her for long minutes, relishing the manner in which she moved her mouth around mine, the way in which her teeth bit my tongue gently.

She was one accomplished babe. She knew all the little nuances. I had thought making love to be a lost art in Red China. She was out to prove me wrong.

My hands went to the dress rolled up to just below her breasts. I drew back a little, lifted the garment. Her heavy golden goody-globes bounced into view. They were big and jutting, the nipples almost an inch long and tinted a very dark red.

I kissed down her throat and onto her left breast. She

cried out, "*Ho t'sai!*" This is a cry of approval in the Chinese. In other words, she damn well enjoyed the touch of my tongue and lips on her jiggling breast and the way I was licking all around her stiffened nipple.

"Do more, do more," she wailed.

I did more. I gathered that nipple into my mouth and sucked it wetly, hungrily. She gave little cries and low moans that aroused me still further. She was no female to stand there and let herself be adored without response. Her perfumed breath panted above my head, her soft palms were sliding around and over my naked shoulders.

I was impatient. So was she. Her right foot planted itself on my left, as she lifted her left leg high, adopting the position of *vrikshadhirudha,* the climbing of a tree, as depicted on the Indian temple carvings at Khajuraho. It was an easy matter to slide into her.

Her hips began a circular movement, ending in a little jerk. The pleasure of this motion is indescribable, when done properly. Ip Chung did it properly, all right. If I'd been any ordinary man she would have finished me in three circles and three jerks.

Instead, her body was the one that convulsed in the sweet death. Her fingernails bit into me, her head hung limp so that her black hair fell down her back to her behind, while her hips thumped and worked and swung. She went off three times like that, yelling out her pleasure every pulsation-packed second.

Her long black eyelashes rose. She stared at me in something like worship. "You have not—burst your cloud!" she exclaimed.

I did not explain anything to Ip Chung, I just hauled her in closer and kept on going.

She sagged against me, after a time, but she clung with her arms and with her *hua-hsin,* her vagina, called flower-heart.

"My leg is tired," she complained. "Please, let us get comfortable. On the bed."

My own legs were a bit shaky so I nodded. I freed myself from her erotic embrace and moved toward the big bed. The covers had been turned down by a thoughtful maid, but Ip Chung ignored them. She plopped herself on her back and raised her thighs, spreading them.

"Come and burst my cloud some more, you wonderful man!"

I slid between her legs. My yang slipped into her yin. Instantly her hips were up and circling around and around in that movement the French name *donner du corps.* Ip Chung had added her own little trademark to the *donner du corps* motion, however, that little bump and grind at the end of the circle. It was enough of a fillup to make me shake with ecstasy.

"You never learned that working in a factory." I grinned down at her. Her eyes were closed, her tiny white teeth were sunk into her lower lip. She shook her head from side to side without looking at me.

"No. I learned in house of happiness."

A brothel. "I thought they were outlawed under the wise guidance of Mao Tse-tung?"

She missed the irony. She panted, "Certain ones for—privileged few—still exist. Not known about in decadent outside world." Her hands were running up and down my sides, and from time to time her long red fingernails scratched my flesh.

"You now—burst your cloud!" she howled.

She was in the orgasmic throes herself, bouncing all over the bed and taking me right along with her. I figured she would be one pooped poppy when this series of *yin chu yangs* were over. She would want to sleep.

I was tired myself. It had been a long day.

My eyes glanced at my traveling clock on the bedtable as she clung to me and her body responses slowed. We'd been at it for an hour and a half. She would be ready for some sack time, too.

No such luck. Her hip motions slowed, but they never quite stopped. And when she realized that my own excitement was still in readiness for another bout, off she went, dancing with her hips and uttering crazy little cries.

If she was out to kill me, she couldn't have done any better. Enough of this four-legged frolic can kill a man. I've known of cases where it has happened in my sexual researches. But my fourpenny cannon was still booming strong, and Ip Chung loved it.

At three in the morning, I pushed her away from me. We'd been going at it since eleven. "I'm beat," I growled at her.

"No! No," she screeched, hands grabbing for me.

I slid away and made it to the floor. My legs were so weak they would scarcely hold me up, so I tottered to the telephone.

"What are you doing?" she asked, lying there with her legs parted lewdly.

"Calling room service. I need sustenance. Especially a drink."

"There's water in the bathroom."

"Water?" I howled.

Funny. She got an odd look on her face, as if she'd made a goof. I take it that she's been carefully taught how best to appeal to a western man, but the Chinese boys who taught her had never been nearer a bar than the Yangtze River. They just didn't know about Old Charter bourbon and all the rest of the bottled stuff.

She closed her legs a little shamefacedly and sat on the edge of the bed. A frown marred her pretty face. "You are not to eat and drink," she stated flatly, as to a lesson well learned.

"The hell you say, honey!"

She got off the bed and ran to me, dropping on her knees. Her soft hands reached for me. I guess she thought she was a real succubus, all right, because she refused to let go until I slammed the back of my hand into her face. I must have hit a cheekbone, because her face was hard beneath her skin.

I said into the phone, "Bring me up a couple of club sandwiches, a bottle of bourbon—make that Old Charter—and a bucket of ice."

She was lying on the carpet at my feet, staring up at me unbelievingly. She did not rub her face. It was as if she had not felt my hand. There was no bruise, either, no swelling of the flesh.

What kind of bimbo had I latched on to?

I said, "Relax, baby. There's no need to rush. You can have some of my bourbon, if you like, even one of the sandwiches."

She shook her head very determinedly. "No, no food, no drink. Just love." On her knees, she began to crawl toward me.

I raised my fist. She halted.

Two tears welled up in her pretty eyes. "You do not like me. I do not please you."

"Sure you please me. Hell, you know that from the way I responded. But man doesn't live by bread alone, honey—nor by screwing. There are other things in life. Like eating and drinking. I'm going to eat and drink."

"No!" she cried, and leaped.

I went backward onto the bed. She was on top of me, her hand scrabbling for my manhood that was still in its proud position. She sought to drop down on it but I twisted away and using a karate chop, caught her across the throat. She fell off me, but she came back strong.

For ten minutes I fought her off. She was inhuman in her animal strength; she was like a female Samson. Her body was not muscular—it was sweetly curved and with all the feminine appendages—but she could scrap like a holy terror.

I had to grab the Venetian blind cords and use them to tie her hands behind her back and her ankles tight together. She still wriggled around but she was forced to lie on the bed and watch me go to the door to get my sandwiches and drinks. Not wanting to let the bellhop see her tied up, I took the tray from him at the door. I dropped a Hong Kong bill for one hundred dollars into his grimy little paw. Or seventeen dollars and forty cents, American.

"Keep the change," I told him.

He bowed almost to the floor.

I went back to the bed, sat on its edge, and began to munch the sandwiches. I ignored the dagger looks Ip Chung was giving me, and the tongue-lashing that went with them. I was called everything from a eunuch to a fag. My manhood was compared to a drooping flower that was dying of old age.

I ate on unconcernedly, but I knew that my temper was gathering strength. When I was halfway through the second sandwich I leaned over and clobbered her left buttock with my hand. She jumped and threw a glance over her golden shoulder at me.

"You want to beat me?" she asked eagerly. "I will let you."

"Forget it," I muttered wearily. "I just want to eat."

I finished half the Old Charter before I figured she was ready to be untied. You might have thought that lying in that cramped position would slow her movements, but no. She whirled and leaped for me, head first and mouth open.

Her moist mouth caught my male flesh. For one awful moment I was afraid she was going to bite. No again. Her soft warmth enveloped me, her tongue went to work and in seconds I was back in the balling business.

There was no denying her this time. Maybe I did not want to, maybe she had gotten to my priapic pride by naming me a eunuch and a fag. I decided to show her I was a sexual superman. She helped with her lips and tongue. She roused me up and then she let me take over.

I began the various positions which Aloysia Sigaea mentions in her *Dialogues*. If I was going to knock out this babe with some knocking up, I might as well have a plan of action. Flat on her back with my hands under her soft rump, I made her adopt the Kentucky posture, with her hips on a pillow and her golden behind raised to my stare as she knelt at the edge of the mattress. I made her turn and lie obliquely across the bed, with her legs to one side, as Caviceo did with Olympia.

I thought I might forget a few positions, but dawn crept through the windows and I was still going strong. The sunlight showed Ip Chung on her side, with me on my side but caught between her thighs. We were going at it hot and heavy, anybody would have thought that it was our first bed bout, rather than about the twentieth.

An hour later I was copying Ovid, having gone through Aloysia Sigaea. My companion was inhuman, I began to think. I had never met a woman who could take the pudendal punishment this one could; usually they collapsed about the fifth or sixth bout. Ip Chung went on and on, slavishly, begging for more and more.

At noon I was almost exhausted.

I was working on the Erotic Postures of Astyanassa, who was the maid of Helen of Troy, at the moment. I don't know whether Astyanassa got her information from that lady or not, she but had them all down on parchment, and I copied them faithfully in the flesh.

At two in the afternoon, I collapsed. I just lay there and let Ip Chung climb on top of me and ride me until I fell asleep.

I admit it. She was too much for me.

For the first time in my life, I had been outdone by a female. For the past sixteen hours—not counting the time I'd spent eating my club sandwich and drinking half a bottle of Old Charter—I'd been in her saddle, cantering and posting up and down, back and forth and sideways. Even my spirit was pooped.

I slept and snored until ten o'clock that night.

When I woke up, Ip Chung was sitting in an easy chair staring at me. I yawned and stretched. "Haven't you slept?" I asked.

She shook her head.

She asked, "Are you ready again?"

"For God's sake," I howled. "Will you get lost?"

She pouted. I turned over and lay face down so she wouldn't get any ideas."You aren't human," I told her. "Any ordinary girl would have been up here with me, snoring away."

Ip Chung just stared at me.

"Well?" I demanded. "Am I Rod Damon?"

"I guess so. I'll report that you are, anyhow. Although you are a bit of a disappointment, you know. They told me you could make love for a week without stopping. I am very sorry. You are not like a virile Chinaman, but I knew that before coming here."

"Now you look here," I snarled, shaking my finger at her pert little nose. "I can out-screw the greatest Chinaman who ever lived. I'll prove it if you bring in a Chinaman and put him to work in the next bed."

Her shoulders lifted in a lazy shrug as if to tell me she couldn't care less about her fellow Chinese, that all she was concerned about was me, and I had let her down. She really got to me, I guess, because my pride was hurt. Nobody but nobody had ever made me say uncle in a love-bout before.

She got to her feet and stretched, letting me see her nakedness in the hope (I assumed) that I would be so smitten with lust for it that I would throw her on the bed again. My eyes met her stare. I smiled and shook my head.

"I've had it, honey," I told her.

She bent and picked up her dress. "Then I might as well put this on again," she told me coldly. She slipped her arms into the blue cloth, then let the rest of it slide down her slimly curved body.

Ip Chung moved toward the door. "So long, fairy."

I threw the sandwich plate after her. It shattered on the door. The Hell with you, sister! Go get yourself bunged somewhere else, next time. I sat there glumly, something like the dying gladiator, and felt sorry for myself.

A woman had beaten me at my own game. She had taken all I had to offer and had come back for more while I'd crept off like a dog with his tail between his legs, howling for mercy. Or just about. My vaunted superiority was a myth as far as Ip Chung was concerned. I was in the dumps so deep I began to think maybe I didn't have priapism, after all.

I thought about going out to some place like the Tsimshatsui district, where the call girls worked. If I could make one of those slant-eyed sweeties say uncle, I would know this was only a temporary thing with me.

I got up to get dressed. A knock sounded at the door. When I opened it I saw a bellhop standing there with a telegram in his hand.

I handed him half a buck and tore open the envelope. There was a couple of pages of typed words, all from Walrus-moustache. The substance of his communique was that the latest word out of Red China, as given by a Thaddeus X. Coxe Foundation agent in Saigon, was that Red China was going in big for robots. Yeah, mechanical men and women. Their vaunted population explosion was a myth to fool the rest of the world.

Instead of half a billion people, Red China had maybe half that. Plenty of hands to do the work, you understand, but not too many to spare for the armies with which Mao Tse-Tung hoped to overrun the world. Since I was going into Red China, it might be a marvelous idea to check on this and let Walrus-moustache know at my earliest opportunity.

I remembered reading about the regimentation of Chinese men and women, in which men have been herded together in compounds and the women in similar concentration camps. There is no mingling of husbands and wives, no sex between them, and so naturally the birthrate will drop. The idea behind this great inspiration of Mao Tse-tung was that the fields needed workers to plant the crops and tend them, and then harvest them.

Crops were needed for food. Maybe Mao also felt that the fewer mouths to eat the food, namely babies, would make more food for all the men and women in their palisaded camps. Now Mao-Tse-tung was reaping these past years of sexlessness. No sex, no kids.

Just recently, a girl escapee from Red China to Hong Kong spoke of shifting populations. I don't mean the Red Guards, I mean the men and women who live in the cities like Peking, Changsha, Foochow. As many as fifty million men and women were being sent into the countrysides, including the young Red Guards. This may have been a plot to explain the dwindling populations to such newsmen who were permitted inside the Bamboo Curtain.

It all began to add up in my mind.

Walrus-moustache might have hold of something.

If he did, it was my job to ferret it out and get answers. Were robots the answer? Had some Chinese scientific genius found a way to manufacture machines to do what a man could do? To hold guns and fire them and man battlefields to attack Russia, Japan, the United States? It might not be so impossible as one might think.

A cold shiver ran down my spine.

I could visualize rows upon rows of spindley metallic things with inbuilt computer banks, fitted out with machine guns and small catapults for hurling hand grenades, moving in unison across a battlefield strewn with dead American soldiers. Bullets would merely bounce off such metal men. If you didn't hit a very sensitive computer spot, protected no doubt by an extra-thick layer of steel, you just couldn't kill such things. There would be no wounded robot soldiers, only disabled ones, so there would be no less for a medic corps.

Maybe they could even program these robot doughboys so that they would blow themselves up like a bomb when they advanced into a group of our boys. The prospect was scary. I thought about Russia and the troubles it had had with Red China at Chenpao Island. Could be that the Soviets had some first-hand information about such robots. Naturally they would keep such information to themselves.

It might be also that with enough robot soldiers, China could hurl itself into an atomic war, realizing that the fallout would not affect their armies in the field. With robots, too, the Red Chinese would not need trucks to carry their soldiers. They could refuel them, when necessary, from the air with a helicopter fleet.

Yeah, the more I thought about it, the less I liked it. Walrus-moustache did right to worry. I determined to find out all I could.

This was no help about my up-tightness on my priapic problem, of course, but it did let me worry about something else. I figured I could get loose by finding myself another girl. As far as the robots went, I would have to wait until—

The telephone shrilled.

A suave voiced asked, "Professor Damon?" It went on, when I identified myself: "I am your contact man in Hong Kong, Chang Li. It is my pleasure to see you, to bring you your passport into the glorious land of Mao Tse-tung, and to arrange for your safe travel."

I figured it would be no harm to be civil. I said, "Praise to your great leader. I am very anxious to do what I can to make Mao Tse-tung understand how much I admire him. When can I expect you?"

The voice was pleasantly surprised. "In ten minutes. I am happy that you feel this way, Professor. I was given to understand that—but then, stupid servants make stupid mistakes."

"I'll be waiting for you," I told the voice.

In ten minutes, a neatly dressed Chinaman in his forties was standing in the hotel corridor, introducing himself as Chang Li while bowing low. I bowed back. He came in and, as Ching Kow had done in my university town, extracted a passport book from his pocket. There was a sheaf of paper money placed inside the book, together with a letter of introduction and a greenish-blue ticket.

"If you permit, I shall be your escort to the river junk, *Pai Lu*, meaning 'White Dew'. Captain Shu Shang is to be your host and captain. It is his duty to make your trip up the Canton river a pleasant one. If he fails to do this, please report him."

I bowed, telling Chang Li that I was positive Captain Shu Shang would be everything Chang Li said he would. "The Chinese are, above all else, most truthful," I added. It was the clincher. Chang Li beamed.

I got dressed under his watchful eye. I expected him to raise a commotion about my Luger that I slipped into my shoulder holster, but he only smiled some more and nodded.

"You must be careful. There are bandits in the interior. It will not hurt to have a gun."

"By the way," I mentioned, "there was a girl in here before, who said she was named Ip Chung. She gave me some sort of sex test, I understand."

"Ah, yes. A test that you passed with flying colors, Professor. Ip Chung was profuse in her praise. She said you were no ordinary sexual giant. You are a carnal colossus. I believe that was the term she used."

"She did?" I asked, gaping in amazement.

His answer was a soft laugh. "She insulted you, you think? No, no. It was merely her way of seeing if you could meet all her challenges. If she showed contempt for your priapic prowess, it was merely to rouse you up some more to demonstrate again how magnificient a man you are."

"Well, now." I grinned, feeling better.

Maybe I would not need a Tsimshatsui district call girl, after all. If Ip Chung was being insulting in the hope I'd bed her down again, I guessed I could forgive her.

"Let's go, Chang Li," I said.

We taxied to the docks from the Hong Kong Hilton. We braked to a stop just beyond Connaught Road Central. This was where the Star Ferries run. There was also a sampan of red paint and teakwood, with a lateen sail flipping in the harbour breeze, riding at anchor.

Chang Li bowed me across the gangplank and onto the deck of the junk. A big Chinaman with a black patch over his left eye and a silk handkerchief on his bald pate advanced with a rolling walk. He was a pirate if I ever saw one. He carried no gun or cutlass, but there was a leather-covered sap tied to his broad leather belt. His blue shirt was open to reveal a heavily muscled but hairless chest.

"Captain Shu Shang, Professor Rod Damon."

Shu Shang said something in Chinese. Chang Li translated it as: "The captain wishes you a long life and a merry one, and wishes to add that while you are his guest you must do everything you wish to enjoy your voyage."

"Just how far are we going?" I asked innocently.

Chang Li smiled. "Into the interior, as far as you can on the *Pai Lu*. Then a car will take you from a small fishing village in Hunan province and deposit you in a village named Tin Song. It is at Tin Song that the purpose of your visit will be made plain. I am sure you know where Tin Song is, if you know your geography, Professor."

"It was my one weakness in school."

He chuckled, delighted. I guess he figured he could tell me any damn thing he wanted, and get away with it. As a matter of fact, my geography is pretty good. I know all about China, Russia, India and Korea, all the "maybe trouble" spots of the world, where I might be sent as a Coxesman.

I heard slapping slippers coming along the deck. Quite casually, I turned my head. My eyes popped.

She was a knockout. Sure, she was Chinese but her face was exquisite, even by movie star standards. Long black hair hung down to her behind and framed a tilted nose, pleasantly slanted eyes, a mouth like a ripe red fruit, and skin the color of a fresh peach.

There was a striped jersey on her from neck to belly-button. Below this she wore blue denim slacks. Her feet were bare except for the flapping leather sandals. Her breasts bounced under the jersey, up and down, up and down, up and down, to her every step. Her hips swung lazily, insultingly, as if she knew that what she had in her blue denim was too much for any man. Especially me.

"Kai Lai, Professor. She is the captain's daughter."

I could not help it. My eyes went to his ugly old face, then back to the girl. Shu Shang was grinning wickedly. Chang Li laughed outright. The girl just stared at me with her charmingly slanted black eyes. She didn't crack a smile.

Not that she was hostile; she just was not about to be gracious. When Chang Li gestured to her, she nodded her head. As she went by, her eyes slid toward me and challenged me. If I ever saw invitation in a pair of female eyeballs, hers were full of it. I dropped my stare to her jouncing buttocks that were almost embarrassingly revealed in the tight blue denim.

"Congratulations," I breathed to the captain.

"Kai Lai take care of you, I assign her to you for—how is it?—for guide on trip. Yes."

I bowed low. "My thanks, Captain. My eternal thanks."

Chang Li held out his hand. "I leave you now. I have other things to do beside enjoy your friendly company, Professor. Farewell for now."

He went dockside, trotting over the gangplank. Two burly

sailors came running to shove the gangplank over onto the dock. Then they cast off. I heard the rattle of the anchor chains. Underfoot, the deck throbbed as a powerful diesel engine thundered into life.

The captain nodded at my glance. "Sail good when wind blows; motor better to make sure junk carry passenger to destination." His one good eye winked. Then he turned on a heel and went off about his duties.

I sauntered to the starboard rail and leaned there, staring at the harbor, at the walla-wallas, those taxi-motorboats carrying their passengers here and there from and to Kowloon Peninsula and Victoria, together with the Star Ferries plying their routes back and forth to the same destinations. It was a peaceful scene. A couple of pretty girls in a Chris-Craft waved bare arms at me. I waved back, admiring their slender shapes in black bikinis.

"You do like girls," a soft voice said.

I turned. Kai Lai stood leaning on the rail beside me. The large red mouth was smiling now, its curves matching the invitation in the glistening black eyes.

She said, "I have heard of you, Professor. I spoke with Ip Chung." She laughed as invitingly as she smiled, I decided.

"I'm not sure my ears didn't burn," I said smiling back.

Her thin black brows rose. "Oh, you must forgive Ip Chung her crudities. She gets very angry when she exhausts a man. She thinks she exhausted you. I do not believe she did. A man tires of too much sex, too fast. Am I right?"

"Ordinarily, I do not tire. But as you say, she came on too fast. Sex is like a glass of water to a thirsty man, it should be sipped slowly and enjoyed."

She clapped her palms together, nodding. "It is so. I have told Ip Chang the same thing, again and again. We shall be good friends, you and I. We think very much alike."

"In that case, we both admire your loveliness very much. You have the same sort of body as Ip Chang, but your face is even prettier. I don't know when I've seen such a beautiful woman."

"Do go on talking. You say delightful things."

My head nodded at the scene around us as the junk gathered speed. "'Right now I would prefer you to act as the guide your father said you'd be to me. The sun is hot, and I prefer moonlight for romance. I'll fill your pretty ears with compliments a little later on."

Her hand rested on mine. The skin was very warm. I lifted her hand to my lips and kissed it. She beamed at me.

"Hong Kong means 'Fragrant Waters Island' in the English," she prattled. "It lies in the South China Sea just below the Tropic of Cancer. It was founded, according to the legend, by a Chinese scholar who sought the most beautiful place on earth for his grave, just about the time when the Normans were invading England under William the Conqueror."

She had a lovely voice, with a sing-song intonation that was melody to the ears. I could listen to her for hours.

Her eyes laughed at me, as if she understood my thoughts. "From that time until the middle of the nineteenth century, this territory belonged to China. Then it was ceded to England. It has been a British Crown Colony ever since. Did you do much shopping?"

"Ip Chung kept me too busy."

Her hand clapped again, that one ringing sound that indicated her approval, I gathered. Every time she clapped, her breasts jiggled enticingly. I decided, staring at them, that I would keep her approving of what I said, as often as I could.

We moved out of the harbor and into the waters of the South China Sea, where the West Lamma Channel runs. To our right—the starboard side—were the New Territories that merged into a series of islands and then the greater bulk of Lantau Island. We steamed into the Canton River estuary and plowed our way through those gray, murky waters until we were making progress up the Canton River itself.

Tin Song lay five hundred miles away.

Kai Lai was a real font of information about almost anything Chinese. She explained quite carefully how the women of China were coming out of the cocoons which they had inhabited for so many centuries. As a mark of their submissiveness, long ago, Chinese ladies had had their feet bound up so tightly that they could hardly walk. Their feet grew distorted by this cramped position, yet were considered beautiful by their husbands and lovers.

As a matter of fact, these deformed feet were usually covered with velvet and satin slippers; it was considered the height of indecency to let a man see them uncovered. The most lascivious caress the Chinese Lady of those years when the feet were bound could bestow on a husband or a lover to take his penis between her hoof-like feet and toy with it.

Today, the wives of high government officials are entirely different than their female ancestors. As female feet have been freed from those intolerable old bindings with the coming of western civilization, so the modern-day Chinese woman was thinking freedom for everybody, Kai Lai assured me, in a kind of sin-suffragette movement. Much of this has been attributed to Siang Ching, the fourth wife of Mao Tse-tung.

Madame Ching has changed the old order. She is a determined woman, energetic and ambitious. At one time she had been an actress, and now she was determined to become the number two power in Red China behind her husband. She is ably seconded by the wife of Lin Pao, Yeh Chun. When Mao Tse-tung dies, Yeh Chun may well become First Lady of China. Today she serves as deputy chief of the army's cultural revolution and as director of the ruling Politburo's military affairs committee.

"There's an old Chinese saying that when women rule China," I said, "then China is decaying."

Kai Lai straightened. "This is capitalistic propaganda! The women of China are its future. Ladies like Siang Ching, Yeh Chun, Tsao Yi-ou and Teng Ying-chao are brilliant in their accomplishments."

Slyly I pointed out that the Hsia and the Shang dynasties crumpled because of too much power in the hands of women, and that it was the Empress Dowager T'zu-hsi who succumbed to the revolt that eventually led to China's going Communist.

Kai Lai was speechless, but she glared at me.

Suddenly she laughed. "Actually, I am not angry with you at all. The mere fact that you know so much of the history of China convinces me that you are an inteligent man. You are not blinded to our past glories. Such a man can be made to see the present and the future glories of my country."

She walked with me down the length of the junk. It was a well-cared-for vessel, the sails were clean and neat, the deck freshly scrubbed. From what I could hear of its throbbing hum, the diesel engine was in perfect condition.

I complimented Shu Shang when we passed him close

beside the forward hatch. He nodded gravely, explaining how his ship was a symbol of the New China, where everything was shipshape. His one good eye twinkled as he spoke, he appeared to look on me as he might on a child. He waved a hand, telling me to enjoy myself.

Kai Lai hooked my arm with hers and drew me toward the bow. We leaned against the port prow rail, watching the riverbanks, which seemed an endless conglomeration of green, growing things, change slowly into tilled and cultivated fields. The sun was ahead of us to the west, slowly sinking. It would be dark in a little while; already the moon was in the sky.

"It is so peaceful at this time of evening," My companion said softly. "It makes me romantic."

I got the idea suddenly that all these Chinese dolls were hooked on sex. Now, I'm all for sex—I make a good living as founder of my League for Sexual Dynamics—but they seemed to be coming on a little too strong. But so automatic are my responses, that I slid an arm about her slim middle and drew her hip closer to my own.

"Too bad we're on your father's ship," I breathed into her ear. She turned a surprised face.

"My father is of the New China, not the old," she exclaimed. "I am a grown woman; I can take or reject a lover as I wish, even on my father's boat."

Her eyes told me she would not be averse to choosing me as a lover. She smiled and laid her head on my shoulder. The offshore wind blew strands of her heavy black hair across my face. They seemed heavily perfumed, excitingly so. I kissed her forehead.

After a moment, she asked, "Would you like to see your cabin?"

"Cabin? I thought I'd be lucky to get a bunk."

Her dazzling white teeth shone in a smile. "You are a guest of the Chinese people. As such, nothing is too good for you." Her shifting hips led the way aft toward the cabin fitted in below the poop deck. This was the captain's cabin, by all rules of the sea. It was going to be mine, apparently for this voyage.

She opened the door. I followed her into a fairly large chamber with windows at the stern through which dying sunlight came in to show me a bunk-bed fastened to the starboard bulkhead, and a table near the right, with a chair. Two hooked rugs were on the floor. Scattered here and there on the bulkheads were nautical instruments, a barometer, a wicked-looking cutlass and two revolvers in worn leather holsters.

It was a utilitarian room; there were no frills.

Kai Lai turned and leaned her rump against the edge of the desk. "We sleep here," she told me, crossing her arms and reaching for the hem of the striped jersey.

I blinked. "We?"

She gurgled soft laughter behind the striped jersey as she lifted it up over her head. Her golden breasts came into view, tipped with dark brown nipples. Chinese women, as a rule, are not noted for their mammary development. Chinese female breasts are hemispherical in shape, and with protruding nipples. While they do tend in later years to become fat and sag, according to Mondiere, when youthful they are extremely shapely.

Kai Lai had breasts that were perfect globes, jutting firmly and quivering to her slightest movement as though set on springs. Jayle has termed such breasts *sein en globe ou globuliforme*. These thoughts ran through my head as Kai Lai straightened and pushed out her *seins* at me.

"Get ready," she smiled. Her fingers relaxed their hold on the striped jersey. It pooled on the floor at her sandaled feet.

I was ready, but I didn't tell her that. I slipped out of my jacket and began unbuttoning my shirt. My body has great recovery powers where love-making is concerned. To look at me as my trousers and shorts came down, nobody would guess I'd ever heard of a girl named Ip Chung.

Kai Lai had the same voluptuous breasts that Ip Chung boasted, and the slimly plump hips, the shapely thighs. Her denim pants went down to her ankles and she stood naked before me. She assumed a proud pose, nude above her sandals, head thrown back. Her eyes raked my midsection, gleaming with pleasure.

"You are a real man," she breathed.

She advanced on me, her hips swinging. Her handsome golden legs bent and she went down before me as the women of Phoenicia are said to have done with their lovers, for the oral congress was well known in the ancient world. Two soft palms came up to hold me worshipfully.

Her eyes raised to my face. She whispered. "We shall love all the night long, and tomorrow, and tomorrow night as well."

I figured she was kidding. She wasn't.

CHAPTER SIX

She came to her feet, sliding upward against my body, her naked flesh to mine, soft and warm, smooth as satin. Her kisses went up my body along with her breasts and belly. When her lips were just at my throat, I bent down and kissed her.

Her mouth was warm, wet. She kissed with hunger in her moving lips and stabbing tongue, with a lazy sense of suspended Time, as if this were all, this were eternity itself. The pleasure built in me until I wanted to yell. Kai Lai was a knowledgeable babe. My hands moved up and down on her bare back. I caressed her buttocks very gently with my palms as I ran them up the lozenge of Michaelis, that triangle of beauty is seen above and centrally located to the buttocks. My fingertips slid down the cleft.

Kai Lai moaned. Her thighs moved together as her hips worked. "Take me," she breathed. "Take me now! I die for the touch of your tortoise head."

"As my tortoise head yearns to sheathe itself in your flower-heart," I replied.

I was in no mood for play. I moved her backward, step by step. When the backs of her knees touched the edge of the bunk, she sat down. Her hands went out to brace her body on the crumpled coverlet. Her golden thighs rose and parted.

The bunk was high off the floor. By leaning forward, I could perform the *hannechi* connection of the Arabs, which translated, means in the way of the serpent. I became a snake, writhing back and forth inside her yin as Kai Lai opened her eyes wide and squealed in absolute delight.

She panted, "Hai, hai, hai!" as her hips worked from side to side, and back and forth. She was as emotional as Ip Chung had been. In a matter of seconds her soft thighs were holding my hips and her ankles were locked at the small of my back.

We went on and on. This Chinese doll must have orgasmed a dozen times, to judge by the intense spasms of her body. Her legs tightened and loosed, tightened again and then parted. The constant *souak el feurdj* movements were a bit much for her. She could not retain her seated posture. She slumped over on her spine.

Her big breasts shook like golden jelly to my copulative rhythms. The *souak el feurdj* motion is a steady movement in and out and sideways, in the wriggling methods of the snake. I do not believe Kai Lai had ever experienced this particular pleasure before, her gasps and cries and stifled words told me it was something new in her experience.

She might have beat her palms together in that odd way she had, but her palms were too busy caressing me, urging me on and on to greater heights.

I was determined to exhaust her, something I had failed to do with Ip Chung. I wanted no insults about my virility from Kai Lai. When I was done with her, she would think me heterosexual Hercules, a potent priapist of that class the Japanese name *dokyo,* after a long-dead priest who was reputed to enjoy the strongest penis in the entire world.

China has its own hard-headed hero, the Hsi Men Ch'ing of the book *Chin P'ing Mei.* He was a notable cocksman. indeed. But I like to think I outdid him this night, with the whimpering convulsing Kai Lai. It is true that I was driven by a kind of need to rebuild my image in my own eyes. No woman was going to make me call quits again the way Ip Chung had done.

I hammered away, shifting my knees to the bunk edge.

"You have the clitoris of the hyena," I panted.

Her eyes were closed, her teeth sunk in her lower lip, yet she parted that red, bite-swollen mouth to say, "Yours is the great yang of the bull! The stallion. Oh, burst my cloud all night long, dear Professor!"

I tried damn hard.

Naturally we lost track of time. Her "tongue grew cold" as the Chinese phrase the supreme delight of the diddled dame, a score of times. The night was dark beyond the cabin windows; occasionally, as we changed positions, I caught the tracery of moonlight on the water of our wake.

And we did change positions, many times. Yet always I so managed my body and hers that my yang was in constant contact with her clitoris. I wanted to exhaust her, to make her crawl away from me, fleeing from my priapism as from the plague. Only in this way would I feel my old true self.

She moaned, "Liu Hiana had you in mind when he wrote his *Lieh-hsien-chuan!*"

Being a complete sexologist in my role as founder of the League for Sexual Dynamics, I knew she referred to the Han scholar who lived in the first century before Christ, who claimed that the male retention of semen preserved the male power and made him young. The *Lieh-hsien-chuan* was his masterwork, dealing as it did with the sexual exploits of Jung-ch'eng.

According to the Chinese erotologists, a man has only a limited amount of sperm to distribute in his amorous exploits; a woman has an inexhaustable supply of ova. Apparently Kai Lai and I were demonstrating the truth of this old axiom, because her cloud burst so many times I lost count while I had not burst my own cloud even once.

Dawn found us in the bunk, me on my back, Kai Lai crouched above me, her hips sliding and stabbing back and forth on my maleness. There were tiny purple rings under her black eyes with their sooty lashes, but she did not heed the tiredness of which they were a sympton.

"More, more, more," she sobbed.

I began to think it was the only word she knew.

Well, I was going to give her more. I was not yet tired, though I must admit to a bit of soreness. I reflected on the many positions explained in the *Jou-p'u-t'uan*, a Chinese erotic classic. I swung over into the Posture of the Butterfly Exploring a Flower, and followed that with the Posture of the Bee Stirring Honey. Kai Lai ate it up. She loved it. Her hips went flying all over the place and she screamed thickly in her happiness until her throat must have been raw.

Sunlight was a golden brightness in the cabin. I was getting damn hungry, not to mention thirsty.

"Can't I have a little wine? Or water?" I begged.

She smiled up at me, being in the position entitled The Starving Horse Races to the Oatbin. She was flat on her back, her legs upraised, the undersides of her thighs against my chest, with her ankles on my shoulders. She held me to her with her fingers widespread on my back. Our tongues were touching, our mouths foraging for kisses.

"Water, of course. No wine," she panted.

I struck while she was in a good mood. "How about some food?" When she seemed to debate this in her head, I added, "You may be on a diet, but I'm not."

Kai Lai nodded, "Very well. Food, then."

Her hands drew me to her again and my stallion galloped as fast as he could to her oatbin. When she peaked, screeching and bumping herself up into me, I held her tightly until she subsided.

Then she pushed me away and padded naked to the door. She did not open the bolted door, she merely yelled, "Bring us a tray with some food on it. And a pitcher of water." She hesitated, then looked over her shoulder at me. "Bring also a little rice wine."

She came back toward me. I would willingly have seen her don her striped jersey and blue denims, but she was determined to have another go at our erotic exercises. Reaching beneath the bunk she brought out a ceramic jar in the shape of a male organ. Sighing, she shook out some reddish powder on her palm.

"Hashish?" I asked, knowing that the drug made the male organ become a stick of jade, indeed.

"Mixed with other things like cinnamon and ginger," she smiled, kneeling beside the bed and reaching for my manhood. Gently she powdered it red, then rubbed in the mixture. My penis began to sting, as if absorbing all the heat from the red powder.

In moments I was as potent as a sexual Samson. Kai Lai gurgled delightedly. She was about to climb up on me again when a knock sounded at the door. She ran to the door, buttocks jiggling, and threw back the bolt. Her hand reached out. Somebody put a tray in it. She used both hands to hold the tray and kicked the door shut with a golden foot.

I went to help her, somewhat ludicrous in my stuck-up state.

The tray was piled with such Chinese delicacies as egg foo young, egg rolls, sweet and sour pork. There was a bowl of gravy on it as well as small offerings of chicken with walnuts, and water chestnuts with kidneys.

"The captain sets a mean table," I marveled.

Kai Lai smiled. "It is in your honor that we have brought

along Ging Tou, who is the finest cook in Canton. He outdid himself this time, I believe."

She took no food and drink herself; she knelt before me and held the tray so I could make my own selections. As she did so, she leaned far forward so I could place the tray on her naked back. This posture brought her lips close to my manhood.

While I feasted above, she feasted below, and when we were done, she knocked the tray aside and clambered up onto my lap. She turned her back to me, planting her bare feet on the hooked rug, and sank down.

"Don't you ever get tired?" I asked, after a time.

"Never of this! I was born for *fang shu,* for bedroom play!"

She was indeed. As I was myself. But enough is enough. Toward three o'clock in the afternoon, my body was trembling with exhaustion. Not my manhood, that seemed to be a different part of me. It clamored for love; it was ready to go on and on. But my every other muscle was finished.

At four, I pushed her away, held her there at the length of my arms. "Go get another playmate," I begged. "We've been at our game of yin and yang for more than twenty hours without a rest. I'm beat."

What am I saying? I asked myself. I was admitting to another defeat at the hands of a Chinese doll! I was quitting under female fire. Me, Rod Damon! The priapist! I could not believe my own ears.

My tongue was smarter than I was, or maybe it was only my subconscious at work. A guy could kill himself this way. A part of me would not let me do that. It had spoken through my tongue.

I could have wept, but I was too tired for that. I held Kai Lai off as long as I could, and then I fell asleep. I was beat, worn to a nub. Whatever happened while my eyes were closed and I was dreaming, let it: At least the rest of my body would be resting.

My eyes opened to lantern light.

I was alone in the cabin. It was something during the night. The diesel engine was trobbing down in the hull and the junk was moving quite rapidly up the Canton River. I yawned, stretched, and went back to sleep.

Kai Lai woke me, kissing me with parted lips. She was

naked again. I had never put on any clothes. I shoved her off.

"I need exercise. Scram!"

"You are a magnificent man, Professor—but you're no superman. I proved that last night."

My hand fumbled for my shorts. "You know somebody who's better, huh?"

"Oh, many men. You'll get to meet them in Tin Song."

"Chinamen all?"

Eyes roguish, she nodded her head until her black hair flew. "All, and for the greater glory of the mighty Mao."

"Hogwash, honey. I don't believe it."

I got into my clothes, found some rice wine still untouched and swallowed it all. It spread through me, warmed me. I needed warming. I was lower than a snake's belly in the confidence department right now. For the second time in something like two days I had failed to make a woman cry, "Enough!" It was a bad feeling.

My feet aimed me at the door. My hand opened it. I walked out on the deck. The river air was fresh, cool. Captain Shu Shang saw me and waved a hand. I went to stand beside him at the port rail.

"We're making good progress," I complimented.

His shoulders shruged. "It is to be expected. My *Pai Lu* is a fine vessel. She carries an important passenger." He grinned at me. "Did my daughter exhaust you?"

"Just about."

I told myself the mores of China were surely changing when a man could speak this way of his daughter. So much for the doctrines of Mao Tse-tung.

We got into a discussion of Marshal Lin Piao and his changes which are marking Peking doctrine. Gone is the fear that held Red China in its grip for the past two years, along with the Red Guards. These adolescent apes have been sent into the country to learn how to farm. They had become a millstone about Mao's fat neck; this was one way to get rid of them.

Trade goods were appearing in the marts of Peking and Shanghai. Not the drab garbs of former years but brightly colored silks and woolens. It was as if Red China had come to realize the depths of its mob madness and was determined to bring back a sense of normalcy.

Was it the real goods, though—or window dressing?

Shu Shang claimed it was for real. He praised Lin Piao as being Mao's right arm and a strong one. Today, Chinese in authority were sitting down with foreign diplomats instead of causing the Red Guards to overturn their cars and do them bodily harm. There was no more burning and looting of foreign embassies. Red China was about to take its place in the world.

I was not so sure. If there were any truth about the robots, it might be wisdom to play down their public belligerency until the world lowered its guard. Then would be the time to send out its robot army across Siberia and into Russia, to let loose their atomic warheads toward Moscow and Stalingrad, and maybe even San Francisco and Los Angeles.

The proletarian cultural revolution was at an end, Red China would have the world believe. Maybe so. But I did not swallow the doctrine that the new era of Lin Piao was all sweetness and light, as Captain Shu Shang would have me believe. Somebody was going to lower the boom one of these days. Then the world would really know and understand Red China.

The *White Dew* moved steadily onward.

When night came, I got into my cabin before Kai Lai could follow me, and bolted the door. She hammered its wood with her fists and pleaded with me to let her in, but I lay back in the bunk, pulled up the covers, and drifted off to dreamland.

Next morning, I felt fit as a bikini on a movie starlet. I ate a breakfast worthy of a gourmet and drank three cups of rice wine. I did miss my coffee, I admit that, but Kai Lai brought me Cantonese tea to make up for it.

She was quite cheerful, I saw. Apparently the twenty-odd hours we had spent in embrace had been enough for her. Or else she considered the bolted door by which I kept her out of my cabin to be a sufficiently strong hint. At any rate, for the next few days she was most circumspect.

When I teased her about having forgotten her needs for *fanq shu,* she giggled. "It was forbidden, after night before last. It would not be fair to you."

"Oh? How's that?"

"We dock soon, at Pong Chi. Then we go overland to Tin Song. We are deep in the interior here. At Tin Song, you will begin the great experiment, to see if you can make love well enough to exhaust Chinese joy girls."

The answer was obvious, her eyes told me. I was quite a man but nobody could exhaust women like Ip Chung or Kai Lai. As if she could read my thoughts, she said, "And we're just a casual sampling of Chinese women."

"You're a little more than that," I accused.

"What do you mean?"

"You're like no women I ever met, and I've met a lot of dames. I've knocked them all out with my erotic endeavors, believe me."

"Not a woman of Red China!"

"Oh, yes." I mentioned Tao Yuan with whom I had traded some yang for her yin on my Kashmir caper to help Prince Setura Khan. "Tao Yuan was no superwoman and she was just as Chinese as you are. As a matter of fact, she was a Maoist secret agent."

Kai Lai looked disturbed. She cried out, "I do not believe you! No man can keep up with a daughter of Mao Tse-tung!"

"I don't know how you do it, baby—but I'll find out."

Kai Lai turned and walked away.

Next day the *Pai Lu* turned toward shore, heading for a long pier standing out from a small town, jutting into the muddy waters. Half a dozen peasants in blue linen jackets and baggy pants, wearing straw cone hats, were waiting there for us. The *White Dew* anchored about fifty feet off-shore. The men in the blue linen suits shoved a shallow-bottomed rowboat into the water. Two of them manned its double oars.

Captain Shu Shang came to stand beside me at the rail. He said pleasantly, "I myself will accompany you, Professor, to the village of Tin Song."

"And Kai Lai?"

"My daughter has other duties that demand her presence elsewhere." He chuckled. "You will not miss her, there will be many pretty girls where you are going."

I moved down the little ladder to a thwart of the row-boat. The captain came after me, practically walking on my heels. He was still very friendly and I began to think that maybe he meant what he said about being my escort. I sat down and the two men with the oars stroked back and forth. They nosed the boat up against the pier.

I stepped up and breathed in the smell of river waters. As I did so, I heard the sound of a car motor. A black touring car pulled up alongside the crowd lining the banks, watching me in silence. A man in a black suit got out and came striding forward.

He bowed low. "Professor Damon? I am Ling Tow, your guide. I am to take you and Captain Shu Shang to Tin Song. If you will be good enough to come with me?"

I went along, with Shu Shang falling into step. We got in the car together and the driver hit ninety traveling along a dusty road toward the small fishing village of Pong Chi. I did some thinking when I could. Ninety miles an hour on a rutted dirt road is quite an experience, however, so my thought processes were somewhat limited.

The Red Chinese wanted me for a reason. I could not swallow the idea that they merely wanted to test the strength of my penis. There was another reason, there had to be. Walrus-moustache wanted me to spy on them, to check for the possibility of robots in Red China. This made good sense. It did not make good sense when I pondered over their invitation to me. What did they have in mind? Certainly not the mere idea of giving me physical pleasure! Nor did the other reason, the idea of screwing me to death with pretty Chinese bimbos particularly apply.

The car stopped before a house.

Ling Tow said, "Please light down, Professor. There is a necessary task yet to be performed before you are ready for your journey."

My shoulders shrugged. I stepped down and went into the house with Ling Tow and the captain. A girl who had been standing in the room into which we walked came forward.

"Is everything ready?" Ling Tow snapped.

The girl made a little bow.

"You will go with her, please," Ling Tow said. "It is very necessary. It is part of your visit."

The girl turned and led the way to another room.

This house I was in was an old one. It held silk screens and very delicate furniture painted with red lacquer and gold. Chinese furniture consists of benches and chairs, for the most part. Some of them were of ebony, inlaid with ivory and lapis-lazuli. A moon window opened onto a garden in the back of the house.

The girl waited until I was in a small bedroom. Then she closed the door and gestured me to the low bed. I raised my eyebrows at her. She did not speak, she came across the room and began undoing the buttons of my suit.

I pushed her back.

"I've had enough loving, honey. I'm waiting for the contest."

She looked puzzled. Then she turned on a heel and went to the door. She beckoned Ling Tow.

"What's the trouble?" he asked. "Yi Lou here is a mute. She cannot speak. She is to undress you and cover your body with a pigment that will make you look like a man of the Chinese republic."

"How come?" I asked. "Isn't my white skin good enough for you?"

"Certainly, my dear Professor. It is just that—"

He frowned thoughtfully. I could read his face as I could a book. His eyes widened in delight as an idea came to him. He exclaimed triumphantly, "However, there are roving bands of Red Guards hereabouts. They hate foreigners. They may stop our car on its way to Tin Song. If they find a white American with us, they will pull you out and execute you very slowly, with sharpened bamboo stakes."

"And you can't protect me?"

Ling Tow shrugged.

I did not believe him for one moment. There was another reason why I should pose as a Chinaman. Bide your time, I counseled myself. Put on a good face and let them do what they want. I put my hands to my jacket, lifting it off.

"All right, I'll go along with you."

Ling Tow went out and closed the door. The girl came for me again, hands outstretched. She wanted to undress me, so I let her. She seemed very detached about the whole thing, there was none of the hot rut about her that had characterized Ip Chung and Kai Lai.

When I was naked, she gestured at the low bed. I lay down on my front. Yi Lou lifted an ointment jar, smeared some gold salve on it, and began rubbing the stuff into my pores. She sat close beside me on the bed, leaning over me. Her breathing was soft, unmoved. Her palms were smooth, gentle.

Those hands lulled me to sleep.

A hand shook me. I opened my eyes. Yi Lou was smiling down at me. She put her hands on my shoulders and tried to roll me over. I got the idea. I turned over and lay on my back.

The girl stared at my loins, eyes wide. I guess the sleep must have refreshed me because my priapism was showing. My manhood was limp but bloated. As Yi Lou stared at it, it started to rise.

She gasped. She turned away her eyes and filled her hands with the ointment. Leaning over me so that her heavy breasts brushed my chest, she began working on my face. Into my forehead and cheeks and ears she rubbed. I found myself staring at the way her breasts bulged out the linen of her jacket. She had breasts like Ip Chung and Kai Lai, round and full. Her nipples were stiff too.

My head reeled. My studies have told me that most Chinese women have small bosoms. The three examples of femininity I'd met so far were just the opposite. Their mammary endowments were almost western, by comparsion. I stared into her face.

She was just as pretty as Ip Chung and Kai Lai, except that her features were subtlely different. A full red mouth, black eyes with long black lashes, glossy black hair that hung down over her shoulders, made her seem almost like a sister to them.

The yellow hands were moving down my neck and chest, rubbing in the salve. She was breathing a little faster as she let her palms and fingers slide over my rock-muscled belly. I have a good body—I need a strong body to accomplish my tasks as a member of the Coxe Foundation. Apparently Yi Lou liked it. She was having a good time with it, rubbing in that golden salve.

When she came to my loins, she drew away her quivering fingers and turned to the jar of ointment. Dipping in her fingers, she started applying more of the salve, directly on my swollen manhood.

"Easy," I said, grabbing her wrists.

I did not want her to weaken me. I knew damn well I'd need all my strength for sex once we got to Tin Song. Yi Lou did not understand. Her wrists turned slowly in my hands. She tugged them to free herself.

Her eyes pleaded with me for understanding. She had a job to do. I must allow her to continue. I allowed her, by releasing her wrists. The notion came to me that all she had to do to free herself was pull free of my hands. The manner in which she had turned her wrists had told me she was incredibly strong.

Puzzle after puzzle. What kind of women was Red China breeding, these days? They were super-sexed, and apparently super-muscled as well. I eyed her more closely. Her body was slim, almost the exact duplicate of the bodies of Ip Chung and Kai Lai. She had no reason to be so strong. For strength, a person needs big muscles. And her muscles were no larger than those of any other girl.

She was still rubbing salve into my manhood. Her black eyes were enormous, staring down at me. You might have thought I was the first man she had ever seen. Around and around my privates her salve-sticky fingers worked. I stared down at myself. From my loins upward. I was the color of a Chinaman. My legs were still tanned white, and somewhat hairy. Yi Lou had not gotten around to them yet. It began to look as if she never would.

"Don't make me lose my yang essence," I warned.

Her lips curved in a gentle smile even as her slippery fingers writhed and stroked all around my jade stick. The Chinese place much store by the yang essence. It is supposed to give longevity if retained during intercourse, and if the yin essence of the female bathes it regularly.

The all but legendary Shou Lou is reputed to have had thousands of wives and concubines, and to have kept them all happy with his phallic prowess. He is always shown with a peach, the symbol of the female private parts, clutched in a hand. Sometimes a dragon, representative of the cosmic yang essence which has risen up his spine to his enlarged head, and which gives him his nearly eternal youth, is shown entwined about his body. At times I have thought that Shou Lou was as afflicted with priapism as I was myself.

Yi Lou bent and kissed me with slightly parted lips. Her tongue ran about my tortoise head in a lazy circling. Her hands that held me squeezed me tight. She was building me up for a bedtime bout, but I was mindful of the tests that were to be held in Tin Song.

Gently I reached out, slid my fingers into her black hair, and lifted her away from her plaything by force. Her pretty face was set in a caricature of sensual joy, which changed soon enough to an angry grimace.

Her lips opened and closed. She could not speak, she was a mute, but her working lips told me that she needed me, that she was going to have me. Her red-nailed hands went to her peasant jacket, ripped it down the front. Big golden globes leaped out to hang before my eyes. Her breasts were almost the exact duplicates of those of Ip Chung and Kai Lai.

"Sorry about this, honey," I said, and swung my unyellow legs off the bed.

She hurled herself at me and wrapped her arms about my chest while she slapped her open mouth on mine. She was really something, rubbing her bare nipples up and down on my chest hairs, panting and sobbing between my lips.

It took all my strength to throw her off. Once again I was reminded of the physical prowess of Kai Lai. I slammed the back of my hand against her jaw and damn near broke it.

I ran for the door.

Yi Lou was right at my heels, silent except for the slap of her slippered feet on the carpets. I bolted for the open air. Yi Lou followed.

I am a good runner. I have run the hundred-yard dash in close to ten seconds. I ran from that house as if the devil were after me with a red-hot pitchfork, but Yi Lou gained on me. I could hear Ling Tow calling after us, with something like pure fury in his voice. I didn't stop to argue.

She caught me under a peach tree, appropriately enough. Those bare yellow arms went around me and we both fell to the ground. Yi Lou was grunting and groaning, scrabbling at her jacket, lifting it off over her head and then putting her thumbs to her thin trousers. They went down to disclose her golden belly and the black brush at her loins.

Naked, she sprang at me again.

This time I was ready for her. I grabbed her right arm, whirled and threw her over my shoulder in the Flying Mare wrestling hold. She thudded to the ground. I expected to see her lying there, broken in spirit if not in body. But Yi Lou was a regular rubber ball.

She bounced up and came for me again.

I socked her in the belly. I hit her on the jaw. She took both punches, grinning, and came on, digging in her bare feet for better traction.

What kind of woman was this?

I was getting scared. No matter what I did to her, it was as if she had not felt it. Her skin darkened where I'd hit, but aside from that she showed absolutely no effects from my blows.

In desperation, I caught her arm again and rode her over my hip, tossing her upside down at the peach tree below which we were fighting. Her left arm, wildly outflung so as to maintain her balance, hit the thick, low branch that almost scraped the ground.

She hit the ground and bounced.

I damn near screamed in horror!

CHAPTER SEVEN

Her left arm had snapped off at the elbow!

I expected to see broken bone and a lot of blood and hear her screeching in agony. Instead she got to her feet and came for me again. My eyes bugged out, I guess, at sight of that stump of a left arm.

There was no broken bones, no blood!

Only wires! They dangled from the stump, jutting out of a hollow upper arm as if she was some kind of machine. I gulped. I swallowed. She damn well *was* a machine. She was one of those robots old Walrus-moustache had told me to be on the lookout for.

"You aren't real," I breathed, backing slowly.

Her movements were even slower than they had been, as if the breaking of her arm had jarred loose other connections inside her skull or chest. She moved like a man under water, almost painfully. But her eyes still glistened and her red mouth went on cooing to me.

Men were running up to us by this time. I saw a panting, sweating Ling Tow following close behind the patch-eyed captain, Shu Shang. They looked fit to kill, glowering at me and at the robot girl who kept coming for me.

"Somebody stop her," I yelled.

Shu Shang was the one who did the deed. He leaped forward, yanking the leather sap from its belt-hook. He brought the sap around in a vicious swing, just at the nape of Yi Lou's neck. There was a crack as if he had broken a ceramic plate.

Yi Lou tottered, emitting sparks from her broken arm. Her eyes rolled up in her head. Her good arm waved around and around like a windmill blade as she twisted sideways, beginning her fall to the ground.

Ling Tow was mopping his wet face as he pulled up beside me. "Terrible, terrible," he kept muttering in a Chinese dialect. "I told them that this would happen. I begged them not to send me defective models!"

"Hey, what's going on?" I asked dazedly, trying not to let him know I understood him.

My words snapped him to attention. His black eyes peered sharply at me. Then his shoulders rose in a casual shrug. His mouth smiled apologetically.

"You were not to know of this as yet," he said ruefully. "It was to be a surprise when we reached Tin Song."

"Maybe I'd better not go on, then," I offered.

His hand whipped out of his coat pocket, holding a small Chinese automatic. His eyes had turned hard. Gone was the professional smile of the escort. "You will come with us, please. If you do not come, you will die here and now."

He looked as if he meant it, so I raised my hands to him, palms up. "Okay, okay." I tried to keep the jubilation out of my voice. Apparently my being in Red China had something to do with the manufacture of the robot women, though I didn't know what. I was being taken to Tin Song by force, so they certainly could not suspect me of *wanting* to go to Tin Song as a Coxeman secret agent.

Just beyond Ling Tow, Shu Shang was glowering at me with his one good eye, slapping his leather sap into his calloused palm. Half a dozen of his bullyboys from the *Pai Lu* were also staring at me, as if daring me to try to escape.

Not me. I smiled at everybody and said, "I'm only too happy to go with you Ling Tow. Just tell me what to do."

Since I was naked and he was surrounded by all those

musclemen off the *White Dew*, he figured he was safe. He put the gun away.

"You will finish putting the golden salve on your legs, please. It is most important that you be a Chinaman."

"Why?"

His sober face shook from side to side. "I cannot tell you that; it is forbidden. You will learn why in Tin Song."

"Okay, let's go back and get it done."

I walked ahead of the little cortege to the house. I cast a glance back over my shoulder and saw one of the sailor boys dousing the robot figure of Yi Lou with gasoline. Then he touched a match to it. The robot body flared with flames.

My head was reeling from what had taken place. I was quite happy to be left alone to finish off my legs with the golden salve. I needed time to think. Yi Lou had much the same body as Kai Lai—and also as Ip Chung, for that matter. Could those two Chinese dolls have been robots too? With a common model for their figures? It was not beyond belief.

But Ip Chung and Kai Lai had seemed so real!

Well, so had Yi Lou.

I never even suspected she was a robot until her arm had broken off against the tree branch. There must have been a ceramic plate at the back of her neck covering some vital part of her wired-up apparatus. A master electrode, maybe, or a diode that controlled her entire works.

In science-fiction parlance, a robot made to resemble and imitate a human being is an android. Those dolls were androids. Somehow the Red Chinese had stumbled onto the processes for making such things. The sweat stood out on my forehead. They were so damned *human!* They could weep and laugh, they held intelligent conversations, they made love like—

I sat up straight. Well, now! No wonder the old *mentula*-master had become exhausted. I'll bet Ip Chung and Kai Lai had been programmed to go on screwing for days, maybe even weeks on end. My ego stirred and got off its can where those bimbos had knocked it. I had stayed with them as no other man had been able to do. No wonder Ip Chung had been so profuse in her praise of me to Kai Lai. I'll bet in her wired-up little mind, I was quite some phallic pumpkins.

I grinned and finished my legs. I reached for a towel and wiped my fingers dry. I felt ready to take on all of China as I opened the door and saw Ling Tow sitting on a bench beside the patch-eyed Shu Shang.

"What do I wear?" I called out.

Ling Tow clapped his hands.

A girl in a quilted jacket and red linen pants came running with the coolie suit I was to don, and a wig of coarse black hair. I drew back unwittingly as she advanced, and Ling Tow tittered.

"Is not need to worry," Shu Shang chortled. "Is real woman."

I took the clothes from her and put them on. Standing in front of a mirror, I fitted on the wig. The result was not too bad. I looked like a Chinese muscleman. My craggy face, handsome enough by western standards, made me seem something out of a Fu Manchu movie.

Ling Tow was delighted by my appearance.

"You make a fine Chinaman, big and husky like the men from Sin-kiang, the desert horsemen. They will be pleased with you at Tin Song."

He rose to his feet, nodding happily. Shu Shang waved a hand, motioning me ahead of them. I walked out into the sunlight and toward the big black touring car.

I sat in front with the driver. Ling Tow and Shu Shang sat in the rear. The driver was a small man, but he could handle that old Daimler as if he were a part of it. We whipped out of the fishing village and along one of the dusty roads at better than eighty miles an hour.

There were bare brown hills all around us on the border of Hunan province, but they gave way to tilled farm fields where we could see men and women working side by side. Under Mao and his collectivism, which included the barracks society in which the sexes have been segregated in separate compounds, the tillable land of China has been in revolt. The famines that beset the people are a result of the chaos afflicting the agricultural administration. Maybe the peasants themselves too, but whatever the reason, the Chinaman has been abusing his soil for more than a decade.

The failure of food crops caused the famines. No wonder the Maoists were turning to robots.

Everything started clicking into place in my mind. If the Chinese could succeed in making robots till the fields as well as fight for them, they would have a force of manpower at their disposal that would be better than slaves. Slaves have to eat, robots do not.

So I watched the workers in the cabbage fields, studying their movements. I had the feeling that the poorer robots would be put to pasture hoeing and harvesting, the better one would get to be soldiers.

The car raced on.

I was struck with an idea. "You know, I haven't seen any dogs around. Or other pets, for that matter. No chickens, no birds of any sort. And crows and sparrows used to abound."

The driver said, "Dead. All dead."

From the back, Ling Tow added, "Many people have been starved, Professor. As you may or may not know, sparrows and crows are eaten by the peasants. So scarce has food been in my country that the bird population has all but been destroyed by hungry people."

"Dogs as well," I muttered.

"Dogs are no exception."

I sat silent for another twenty miles, then said, "You had a big thing going about steel production, back a few years. Backyard furnaces were to smelt it."

"The steel was worthless. It had cracks and bubble holes. The same with our cement." Ling Tow chuckled. "I tell you all this because it won't make any difference whether you learn these facts or not.

"We are not a technological society, and unfortunately this is a technological world in which we live. Our alarm clocks are off the proper time by as much as three hours. Our thermos bottles blow up when hot liquids are poured into them. Locks will neither lock nor open. Our hydroelectric works operate at less than seventy percent efficiency, when they operate at all."

"But you've learned to make robots."

"Ahh, yes. It is our one great success. Only with robots can we hope to match the capitalistic powers and that great country, Russia, which is veering more to the west and away from the doctrines of Marx and Lenin every day."

"Maybe they're smarter than your boys."

"It is the goal of all true communists to spread their doctrine across the entire world. This includes Europe and America. With the robots, we hope to be able to do this."

"Since you're in such a good mood," I said cheerfully, "maybe you'll tell me the real reason why I'm here."

"In good time, Professor. In good time."

We whirled through the main street of a tiny town that consisted of a cluster of shacks with some old people sitting before them, staring with wide eyes at the car as we sped past in clouds of dust. Soon the bamboo and thatch homes were behind us, and the suffering eyes of the old people—whose ribs damn near protruded through their skins—were gone.

"How do they stand such a life?" I asked.

"There's always the foot vote," growled the driver.

"Foot vote?" I asked.

"He means running away, Professor. To Hong Kong or to some other place where the word of Mao Tse-tung is not law. He should not speak so. It is high treason."

"I say it because is true picture," the driver protested.

"And because I am a very lenient supervisor," chuckled Ling Tow. "Many supervisors are unsure of themselves, Professor, and so they bear down heavily on the people assigned to them. Me, I feel I get more by honey than I do by vinegar. However, my administrative duties do not extend into Tin Song. There, and please accept this as a note of friendly warning, you will not be allowed to gossip with the personnel."

I filed the note away in my memory.

At dusk we turned off the main highway and slid between rows of dwarfed trees and green fields toward a big cliff that was part of the Chuan Hills. It formed a great escarpment, and its face was dotted with the dark holes of many caves. On top of these cliff faces, green grass was growing, intermingled with trees.

The caves reminded me of the Buddhist cave temples between Tihwa and Kashgar, which have been the subject of study by archeologists. When I said as much, Ling Tow chuckled complacently.

"You continue to surprise and delight me, Professor. Not many westerners know about the cave temples. Well, the caves at which you are staring are also temples of a sort. Modern temples, Professor, where the gods of technology are properly worshipped."

The car raced on. The cave mouths grew larger. I could

make out just inside them objects on which the dying sunlight glinted. Below many of the cave entrances, and stretched across the face of the cliff, were a number of wooden galleries from which the paint and lacquer had long since faded.

Noting my interest, Ling Tow said, "Those galleries are very rare today. They were built by Buddhist monks long ago, actually during the fourth century after your Christ. For more than fifteen hundred years they lay undiscovered, like the Mai Chi Shan grottos at Lung Men.

"And as at Lung Men, we have been uncovering caves rich in art treasures, and in the sculptured forms of the many Buddhas in the grottos."

"I don't get it," I said. "Why bring me to a lot of Buddihist caves?"

"There are Buddhist caves,—Professor and Buddhist caves. Now these are being used for something else. As to why the great Mao chose Tin Song and its cliff caves, permit me to say that they are most secret. No one can get in here to spy on what we are doing. Those caves are safe even from your country's satellites that whirl around the Earth taking pictures of everything that goes on."

"We aren't all that nosy," I argued. "We just want to make sure you and Russia aren't going to bury us, as Nick Kruschev threatened."

"Such nonsense!" he exclaimed, but with a hint of triumph in his voice. Red China *was* going to bury our western civilization, his tone of voice said, but we would not realize what was happening until it was an accomplished fact.

The car pulled up before a wooden staircase that went up along the side of the cliff to the first of the several galleries tiered across the face of the cliff. The steps were new, but the painted galleries were very old. Ling Tow, Shu Shang and I got out. The driver moved the car forward until it was hidden inside a sort of big carport that was camouflaged by its sodded roof to look, from the air, like a stretch of grassland.

I went up the stairs first, followed by Shu Shang, who was along to act as a kind of bodyguard, I gathered, for the smaller Ling Tow. I was not going to try anything stupid. I wanted in on the robot factory that these caves hid from spying eyes and satellite cameras. They did not know this; they were merely taking no chances on my trying to run away.

At the first gallery I was met by a Chinese soldier in quilted jacket, cap, and an AK-47 automatic rifle. He saluted Ling Tow, then chattered at him in a dialect I did not understand.

Ling Tow said, "They are waiting. Come!"

I walked along behind Ling Tow, with Shu Shang and the soldier bringing up the rear. The gallery doors opened onto a series of caves lighted by electric lights, very up-to-date. The grotto walls were painted to represent the life of the Gautama. Judging from the scaffoldings here and there, the finest Chinese artists were restoring those paintings with fresh pigments.

Ling Tow walked past these ancient treasures with a calloused air. He had seen them before, and there was no streak of artistry in his makeup. They were not functional. They could do nothing to increase the lot of China in the modern world; therefore, they were useless to him.

He came to a stop in an office made from a small cave. It was air-conditioned, and there were two desks set across from each other. Ling Tow went to one of the desks and rang a bell.

We waited about five minutes. Then two white men came into the room, staring hard at me. They were Russians. One was blonde and beefy, the other blonde and wiry. They were in their middle forties, I should judge.

One of the Russians said in crude Chinese, "Have him strip. We want to examine him."

"What about Kang Chow? As director of the Chinese Peoples Republic and as coordinator of this entire system, shouldn't he be here?"

The beefy Russian smiled, "He will, he will."

"Now look," I said.

The AK-47 jabbed me in the spine. I shrugged and put my hands to my coolie jacket and yanked it off over my head. The two white men studied my deep chest, the musculature of my arms and shoulders. They nodded, glancing at each other.

"He is a splendid specimen," the smaller man said.

I pushed my trousers down and stood naked. The white men gawked at the size of my phallus, hanging almost limp and casual between my thighs.

The smaller Russian said, "We ought to get a girl here.

I've heard stories about this one's potency, but I don't believe them."

"All in good time," chuckled Ling Tow.

A lean, tall Chinaman in a lab smock came into the office. His black eyes raked me from toes to black wig. Then he advanced on me, hand outstretched.

"Professor Damon, this is a pleasure. I am Kang Chow, director of——"

"I know, I know," I told him, gripping his hand.

He beamed. "You have been awaited eagerly at the Robot Development Center."

"Robot Development Center?"

He explained. "This is where we manufacture such creatures as Ip Chung and Kai Lai." His eyes twinkled. "I do hope you found them everything a girl should be?"

He spoke with a Harvard accent. Later I learned that he had been educated at Harvard and at the Massachusetts Institute of Technology. He had been born in San Francisco thirty-seven years ago. At first enthusiastic about his role as a scientist in American society, he had gone back to China upon the offer of a million dollars and a post in the scientific accomplishments of Mao Tse-tung.

When I got to know him better, I was damn sure it was the offer of the million dollars that made him return to Peking. He was a money-pincher; to him, gold was god. As director here, he got a damn good salary. He banked most of it, since his room and board at the Robot Development Center was for free. I think he had it in the back of his head to amass a fortune and then to get the hell out of Red China before it destroyed him.

I complimented him on the girls. Kang Chow smiled toothily. His hand gestured at the Russians. "They did all the brain work, really. Have you met—? Oh, then let me introduce Fedor Novotny."

The beefy man stepped forward, offered a hand as big as a small ham. I felt his strength in his hand-grip, I told myself not to mix it with this one if I could avoid it.

Kang Chow said, "And this is Dmitri Kolsikoff."

The smaller man merely nodded. In clipped tones he said, "Let's get down to business, shall we? Here is your professor. We see him as a Chinaman. Are his bodily proportions satisfactory?"

Kang Chow nodded. "Eminently so. Novotny?"
The big Russian nodded. "Yes, he will do nicely."
"May I ask what I'll do nicely for?" I asked.
Kang Chow smiled. "You have been selected, professor Damon. Perhaps a demonstration will suit your purpose better than any words of mine."
I went with him, the two Russians at our heels, through the office and along a cave-tunnel into a magnificent chamber filled with all sorts and manner of computers. Big ones, small ones, all with their relay system lights flashing on and off. These machines, explained the director, did the intricate mathematical equations and figured out the proper chemical formulas needed to perfect their robots in their various accomplishments.
"The science of robotics—or cybernetics, as some prefer to name it—has become most delicate and demanding. I don't know how closely you followed robotics back home, but surely you must know that your University of Texas is making robots that will have distinct personalities. They will love, fear, and hate. At Leland Stanford, they are making robots which can see and hear, move around obstacles, plan ahead with as much intelligence as the human brain itself. Other institutions have developed man-like muscles for robots.
"In England, robots are taught to read. An English inventor built a robot that was best man at his wedding. It even kissed the bride.
"Here, thanks to the genius of our fellow comrades Novotny and Kolsikoff, we make robots that can do whatever a normal girl can do." His lips twitched. "Some of them have been programmed to talk and think and to make love almost incessantly—as you no doubt know."
I grinned a little shamefacedly.
"There is nothing miraculous about all this, it is merely an extension of the engineering that produced robots in your own country where they have been used as metal-stampers and die-casters. We go a tiny step farther than your own cybernetic engineers. We give our robots perfect human bodies."
He clapped his hands.
Half a dozen girls ran out of a nearby cave-mouth door.

They wore the linen jacket and trousers of the Chinese peasant woman.

"Strip," said Kang Chow.

The girls undressed, in various shades of confusion. One or two were quite bold about it, three were shy. The sixth girl did a kind of Minsky strip-tease. I heard Kang Chow whisper, "They undress in the manner to which they have been programmed, each with her own distinct personality, you see."

I stared at six naked female bodies that were identical, as far as I could see. Each girl had the body of Ip Chung and Kai Lai. There was no mistake about it. The heavy breasts, the slightly pouching belly, the handsome legs with the plump thighs, were as I had seen them. There was hair on four of the mounts at which I stared, as seemingly real as that on top of their heads. Two of the girls had shaven mottes.

Their eyes flirted with me.

"It is important to a strong male secret agent to be able to make good love quite often, eh? You yourself are the living proof of this. We need such a robot for our own use. Your name was suggested by Tao Yuan. You remember Tao Yuan from your recent exploits in India? She hates you, yet she loves you in her own way, because of your admirable gifts.

"We are going to make many of you, Professor. Each man will have an individual face. Each girl you are looking at has her own face, as a result of the artistry of Chan Dok, one of our fellow workers, as well as her own personality, despite their similarly constructed bodies. We could throw about ten thousand of these girls into the world, if we so wished. We prefer to wait until we have the male robots to accompany them.

"Come along, please."

He brought me to a vast cave that was filled with the bodies of faceless girls lying in freezers. The bodies were those of Ip Chung and Kai Lai, apparently the two Russian robotic geniuses had searched long and hard before they decided on a female body that was five stars and then some where it came to shapely sexiness. They had not given these robots faces, nor activated them, as yet. They lay there with round blobs for heads, without any features but eyes. And all those many eyes were shut.

"Our manpower pool, Professor. Or should I say—girl-power pool? It really makes no difference."

"What about those people I saw tilling the field? Were they robots too?"

Kang Chow shrugged. "A few of our earlier experiments. They are all right as workers, but they are limited to that. This project has been going on for about five years, ever since Novotny and Kolsikoff defected to Maoist China. We use the inferior ones for menial labors, no more."

Like Yi Lou in that little fishing village. Maybe they'd forgotten she had the body of Ip Chung and was programmed to get hot and want to make love upon temptation. My bared manhood had been temptation to set her off. If her arm hadn't broken off, I might never have known she was an android.

"All right," I said, pretending good fellowship, "where do I go from here? What do I do first?"

Kang Chow laughed. "I'm really surprised at you, Professor. We are not barbarians. We will not fling you on a table, strap you down, and go to work on your magnificient body. No, no. You have been seeing too many Frankenstein movies of late. Girls!"

They came running, their bright eyes dancing with mischief. It was hard to believe they were not real live China dolls. Kang Chow stood back and let them crowd around me.

"They will take your measurements, professor. I give you as many days as you need for the task. Isn't that fair? And you'll be wined and dined in one of our most luxurious suites."

"Nobody could ask more," I replied, hugging a couple of girls to my naked body. They giggled and rubbed their smooth skins against me. A couple more came up in front, two more crowded in to my buttocks. Their hands seemed to be everywhere.

Kolsikoff coughed behind a hand. In his dry voice he said, "Before this gets out of hand, there are some further things I'd like to know about our subject."

"The interrogation room, Kang Chow nodded, of course. I'll leave you folks now. I have duties of my own to perform."

He bowed out. The girls and the two Russians walked with me into a corridor and to a room fitted out like a medical office. I must say the Red Chinese had really outdone themselves in this cave compound. Thanks to the air-conditioning and heating systems that blew air all around them, they had made these caves into something out of a science-fiction movie.

I sat down and the girls grouped around me.

Kolsikoff asked questions. Novotny punched some computer cards when I answered. I told them all about myself—except for a couple of Coxe Foundation secrets. Hell, they knew all about me. They had not selected me as a pig in a poke. I just repeated what they already knew.

Every computer has its in-put system. Into this is fed the programming punch-cards with the data necessary for the proper functioning of the computer, things like dates and names and suchlike, together with the instructions as to what the computer is to do with this information. Sometimes an electric typewriter is hooked into the computer, sometimes the computer uses a roll of tape; occasionally, another punched card carries the answers.

Each computer has its own arithmetical unit, its control system, its answering device. The computer is directed to store knowledge or use that knowledge in a process of mathematical reasoning and answer any questions given to it, to print any answers that are needed. They no longer use huge banks of vacuum tubes in computers. Nowadays they depend on miniaturization of its many parts, so that the computers are not nearly as large and as bulky as they once were. The transistors and diodes, sensing-wires and grids, do not take up much space. And these computers are so ingenious that they are being used to train students to be doctors.

Novotny and Kolsikoff got everything out of me they needed. Novotny handed one of the girls a tape measure. He said, "Get his measurements down on paper for us. We will be busy getting all the information we've just taken into our computers' memory banks."

The girls nodded happily. They drew me from the chair where I'd been sitting and, with a girl leading the way—her naked buttocks wigwagging at me in a code I understood only too well—I was led out of the medical section into the living quarters.

The living quarters were up two flights of stairs. Apparently these caves were honeycombed with stairs and corridors, hollowed out of solid rock by Chinese workers and fitted with the stairs and carpets, smoothed-off walls and such in which I now found myself.

My room was circular in shape with wooden walls and wall-to-wall carpeting. Indirect lighting showed me a king-sized bed and cushions thrown around on the floor. The room was about twenty feet in diameter, big and spacious. A writing desk and chair was across from the bed. Bookcases had been built into the walls and held books in English. For my perusal, no doubt.

The girl with the measuring tape stepped up to me so that her hard nipples scratched my chest and her pubic hair tickled my main attraction. She put her bare arms about me and used the tape to measure my chest. I had all I could do to stand still, because the other girls were caressing me with their soft palms, just about everywhere. Only one thing bothered me. My phallus lay limp like dead.

"Forty-three," the girl read. "Now please inhale." She measured me again, staring down at my limp penis with arched eyebrows as she came closer. "Forty-eight. My, you seem to be quite unmoved by all us girls. And I'd heard such things about you, Professor!"

Oddly enough, these girls were not turning me on. Maybe it was because I knew they were robots and not the real thing. Hell, I was no kook who got his kicks from balling clothing dummies. I function only with the real thing. Ip Chung and Kai Lai had been exceptions; I hadn't known at the time they were androids, I honestly believed them to be real, live girls. These are not women, they are machines, my mind was telling me, no matter how good they look. So my phallus folded like a long balloon with a slow leak.

Maybe these girls were robots, but they sure were programmed to act like real girls. They clustered around me, petting me, their soft red mouths kissed my flesh wherever they could reach. It was no go. It was less than effective.

Tape-measure Tilly was kneeling, putting the tape about my upper thigh. This naturally brought her into close contact with my drooping spirit. Her eyes blinked, she made her lips pout. As she drew the tape measure tight, she loosened her lips and leaned to kiss my limp but bloated flesh.

Her face crumpled in dismay. She looked up at me.

"What's the matter with you? You are supposed to boast a super-phallus. What did we do wrong?"

For a moment I was afraid she was going to cry, but she pulled herself together long enough to snap, "Ah Fong, go tell the masters about this. It is very important to the success of the project."

Ah Fong stared daggers at Tilly, but she padded off. I gathered that Tilly was some sort of sub-commissar in the caves. A superior sort of robot, that is. She went on measuring me, that was what she had been ordered to do, but she shook her head from side to side and gave sorrowful little sighs.

The other girls set themselves the task of reanimating my spirit. Their lips kissed me from mouth to toes. Wet tongues were dragged over my chest, my belly, my unstirring manhood. I stood there like a naked golden god and let them do whatever they wanted. My mind was in control and my mind told me these were not real babes at all.

Novotny came himself, with Ah Fong a little ahead of him, half running. Her arm came up, her finger pointed at my collapsed cannon.

The big man shook his head worriedly. "What's wrong? I thought all these girls would have you in fine fettle. Can it be you've had too much fun the past few days, Professor?"

"Not at all. These things aren't real females. My sex habits have been processed since the age of puberty to function only with honest honeys."

"This is a development we hadn't counted on. We were so certain. . . ."

He brightened suddenly. We shall test you with a real girl, Professor. In that way, we can see if you are honestly tired or really do have a thing against making it with a robot. Are you finished, Ming Mei?"

Ming Mei was Tape-measure Tilly. She was placing the tape about my forehead. "Not yet, sir. But soon."

"Never mind the measurements. The other is more important. Come along with me, Professor. We must make arrangements."

I was taken to a room fitted out with a bed and carpet, and a row of seats on tiers like at a theater in the round. I was told to wait, so I lay down on the bed and put my hands behind my back. I fell asleep.

I woke in a dim blue light to the touch of a tongue running over my phallus. A woman was crouched on the bed, kneeling above my loins. Her red tongue was performing the rite of *reparer les torts de la nature*. Back and forth she dragged her tongue on my flesh. My flesh remained quiescent.

My eyes took in the men seated in the tiered chairs and staring down at us. I saw Kang Chow between Novotny and Kolsikoff, as well as half a dozen other men in lab smocks or the hospital wear of medical men. My eyeballs wandered to study the woman kneeling beside me.

She looked real enough.

Her black hair was long and uncut, it half hid my loins, above which her head was poised. Her profile was exquisite, with tilted nose and full mouth and cheeks like peach fuzz. Her breasts were somewhat heavy, though not so large as those of Ip Chung and Kai Lai. Her hips were slender and her legs very shapely.

"Stop," said Dmitri Kolsikoff.

The girl drew back, turning her head to stare at the men. She made an appealing sight, squatting on her haunches. Her nipples were quite long and stiff, so apparently she herself was not unaffected by what she had been doing to me.

The men were going to have a consultation about me. They crowded together, talking in low voices. I gathered that I was one huge disappointment to them all. I had failed them in my very first test. They had to do something about that, like make adjustments.

Novotny glanced down at me from time to time though he was listening to the others. He apparently wanted them to do one thing, they were against his suggestion and proposed a different course of action.

Finally Kang Chow said, "Fetch Mah Tung."

Mah Tung was a middle-aged man who wore the white hospital smock of a doctor. He held a hypodermic needle in a hand. He came to my side with a nurse at his heels. The nurse dipped a piece of cotton in some liquid and massaged my upper thigh. Then Mah Tung stuck the needle in me.

He stood back with a bland smile to wait results.

Nothing happened.

Fedor Novotny slapped the flat top of the railing behind which he was sitting. "You see? It is as I have claimed. He has a compulsion not to make love with a women he thinks or knows is a robot. There is nothing there to stimulate his priapic impulses."

"Then all this is for nothing," Kand Chow wailed.

Novotny shook his head back and forth as he grinned. "I would not say that, no. If you listen to me, I will make him practically rape that girl!"

He rose to his feet and came down the steps into the little round arena where the bed was placed. He walked up to me and lifted out a gold watch from his pocket.

He swung the watch back and forth.

Naturally, I knew what he was doing. I have used hypnotism myself in my League for Sexual Dynamics classes at the University. There were even times when I have autohypnotized myself.

I said, "You can't go around hypnotizing the robots you build that resemble me."

"Possibly not, Professor. They will be programmed however, if this plan of mine works, to make love just as eagerly to robot women as to real women. If we can build them perfectly enough, there is no reason why robot men cannot mate with robot women and conceive children."

"Ohhh, brother!"

His smile was hard. "Look at the watch, Professor. If I can hypnotize you into believing Feng Ti is a real woman, I will know that your robot duplicates will be able to be programmed properly. What is programming but hypnosis of a sort? Now watch the watch."

I did like the man said.

And then I heard him speak.

"Feng Ti is a real woman. She has lovely breasts and a bare body that will hold you in an embrace that will delight you. The touch of her hands and her lips, her tongue, is wildly exciting to your manhood. Feng Ti is a real woman. She has lovely breasts. . . ."

The voice droned on.

The watch swung back and forth.

CHAPTER EIGHT

Soft lips spread upon my own. A tongue slithered into my mouth. I felt naked female flesh on me, grew aware that big breasts were mashed to my chest. A pair of dimpled thighs were moving back and forth with my erection held between them.

Feng Ti whispered into my open mouth, "I adore you, Professor. Please be kind to me. Please, please. . . ."

My hands went up her soft back, stroked down to her plump buttocks. My mind thought of nothing but this naked woman lying on top of me. Vaguely I understood that she was named Feng Ti, that she was the wife of a doctor at a Hong Kong hospital, that her husband neglected her for the embraces of a young nurse on his staff.

I had met her at a ball given for some diplomats. We had flirted with one another, she had been in a lowcut evening gown and enjoyed my staring down the vee to her unbrassiered breasts. We had danced and had made an appointment to meet in a hotel room.

We were in that hotel room now.

My phallus had grown as she undressed for me, pulling off her street clothes, her girdle and stockings. She had turned her back so I might remove her brassiere. Then she had undressed me.

Now we were naked in bed together. There was no rush about what we were going to do; we could take our time. Her husband had left Hong Kong for a Tokyo consultation. Mrs. Feng Ti was free for the next few days until his return.

My fingers sank into her soft behind, urging her upward. She lifted herself and slid up on my body until her heavy breasts dangled inches from my mouth. I kissed each long brown nipple, I took each nipple into my mouth. I played at baby to her breasts while she whimpered and shook above me.

Instead of being held by her thighs, my *peos* was now between her knees. She was making movements with her hips, quivering and shaking at the sensual feelings racing through her flesh. My mouth suckled her hanging breasts gently and hungrily. It had been a long time for the old professor, between girls. Something like a month or six weeks, I vaguely understood.

Feng Ti was going to reap the benefits of my abstinence.

I was so hard and big that I hurt.

My phallus needed the salve of satiation from the sweet yin of this married woman. Her perfumed breath panted in my nostrils as I suckled her nipples, as my hands went around her soft, smooth buttocks and up and down their crease. She whispered words of adoration for the size and rocklike strength of my phallus between her knees, urging and begging me to give it to her, she needed it as she needed the very air she breathed.

My hands moved her upward still more. I kissed a path from her hanging breasts to her soft belly. Suddenly it dawned on her that I wanted to worship her just as she worshipped me with words. Eagerly she scrambled up my body until she was sitting on my hairy chest. Wantonly she parted her thighs and leaned forward.

With lips and tongue I adored her femininity.

Head thrown back, Mrs. Feng Ti wailed her delight to the hotel ceiling. Her body trembled, her hips quivered, afraid to move too strongly for fear of dislodging my lingual caresses. She could not control her bodily convulsions for long, however. A pair of soft inner thighs clamped my head, her hips looped and darted as she began to scream.

I pushed her up and back. I fell between her still-parted golden thighs. My furious priapus drove deep within her inviting flesh.

There is a saying among the Chinese that a woman enjoys "forty times in and out," in which her clitoral bud is stimulated by the friction of the male member and during which she enjoys more than a dozen orgasmic convulsions. Feng Ti did her forty and more, because I was wound up tight as a drumhead and fed her enjoyment as from an inexhaustable fountain.

I went on and on. Forty became eighty, a hundred and sixty and even more. We sawed back and forth like a couple of lumberjacks working at a tree.

Hindu women go for the "nine times shallow, one time deep," so I varied my coital movements to include that particular delight. Mrs. Feng went wild over it, and under me. When I figured she might be getting bored, I grabbed her by her hips and dropped on my back, swinging her on top of me.

Now we could indulge in the corkscrew methods of the Japanese, those circular grinding motions that allow the vaginal muscles to contract about and milk the male intruder. Pretty Feng Ti was out of her skull with ecstasy. Her eyes were closed, her teeth were biting her lips until they damn near bled. The breath was going in and out of her mouth so as to make the *hsa! hsa!* sounds that indicate female enjoyment.

Time stood still in our hotel room. It was as if old Shou Lou was giving our *fang shu* his blessing. My hips went up and around, Feng Ti ground her own hips in a counter-circular movement to match my own. I became the "crystal infant" of ideal Chinese copulation, in which I retained my yang essence while being bathed with the benificent properties of the yin moisture.

Then everything turned into nightmare.

Somebody yelled, "Enough, enough! We are satisfied!"

He was satisfied? I was not.

I snarled and dug my fingers into the smooth golden hips of Feng Ti. She reached down and dug her long red fingernails into my shoulders as if to help maintain coital contact. Hands caught at her—I saw them clearly. Hands also sought to rip me loose from her delightful flesh.

"Get away!" I howled, positive I was going mad but determined to go down struggling. "Get the hell away!"

After a time, the hands slid off.

Feng Ti and I went on and on. There was a malleatic madness in me that caused me to need this furious fluttering (induced, I later realized, by the hypnotism that made me think Feng Ti was a married woman and that I was in a hotel room). I had to thrust my hips upward, I had to grip her hips and make sure they ground and circled above me.

My hands slid along her smooth thighs, caressing her. She felt my palms and leaned her exquisite face down and touched her open lips to my mouth. We kissed a long time, a long time.

But not long enough. Bigger hands came to grab my legs and arms, to yank Mrs. Feng Ti bodily off my jade stick. I howled like an Irish banshee at this deprivation. I struggled upward, ready to fight.

More hands came, this time with a hypodermic needle.

The hands stuck the needle into my arm.

I went out like a broken light bulb.

When I came to, I was in my own room, the round bedroom that had been assigned me. I was naked under the covers, and asleep. My eyelids rose, I stared around the room. Memory came back to me, with understanding.

They came for me when I was up and dressed in the loose linen coolie jacket and trousers. I suspected they had a tiny television camera hidden somewhere in my room. Or maybe it was only bugged for sound.

Novotny and a pretty Chinese girl escorted me to breakfast. The girl was Lee Chi, as pretty as Ip Chung and Kai Lai, and just as well built. Novotny told me that Lee Chi would be my official hostess from there on in, and would relay orders to me from my hosts. Intelligence sparkled in her black eyes, and her smile was happy. She seemed like one of the better robots.

She fed me ham and eggs and coffee, plus some sweetbuns, in the communal dining hall. I ate in solitary splendor. Lee Chi assured me that everybody else was up and working hours ago.

There were no working orders for me yet. I suggested we take a walk, that she show me the layout of the caves and laboratories. Lee Chi frowned, then nodded.

"I have not been forbidden to do so," she stated. "Besides, there is no way for you to escape from here, so it makes no difference."

"Why can't I escape?" I asked.

"The metal grilles come down on the throwing of a switch. They lock into place and can only be opened by the director himself, Kang Chow. You would like to see them?"

I told her I would. I did not intend to stay here a prisoner the rest of my life if I could help it, and I could help it by learning just where and how these metal grilles operated. Lee Chi showed me a control box in the office where I had first met the Russians. That moved the grilles up and down electrically.

The grilles themselves were set into the overhang at each cave mouth. Standing under them, I could glimpse the bright metal of the grille bars recessed into their metal sheaths. We strolled the galleries so that I could see the panorama of this corner of Hunan province stretched before us.

The air was cool and sweet. A steady wind blew across the cultivated fields and over the ribbon-like roads at which I stared.

A loudspeaker blared to life.

"Attention, Lee Chi. Attention, Lee Chi. The American professor is to be brought to the duplication room at once. The American is to be brought to the duplication room at once."

As we were leaving the rickety wooden gallery, I noticed a switch set into a recess. "What's that?" I wondered.

"It is a safety measure. In case some malfunction should lock the grilles in place, a radio call from the laboratory compound would permit someone on the outside to swing this switch and raise the grilles. Otherwise, those metal bars might keep us all inside the caverns until we starved to death."

Yeah, hey! It was a thought I tucked into the back of my head.

Then Lee Chi walked me to the duplication room and sat down, crossing her legs and folding her hands in her lap. Fedor Novotny and Kolsikoff were already in the laboratory, busied over a blue metal table, adjusting a series of searchlights so that they focused on the tabletop.

The beefy man turned from the table and came toward me. "Professor, if you are ready?"

I nodded, knowing I had to play my role to the hilt so as not to arouse suspicions. I stripped naked at his order, I let them put me down on the table and strap my body so that I could not move. They put plastic hemispheres, hollowed out, over my eyes to protect them from the rays of the searchlights.

I heard the click of a switch.

Heat bathed my body; not intolerable heat, just pleasant warmth. All I knew of what was happening now was that heat. Later, Lee Chi explained this process more fully to me. The searchlights were highly modified ray-probes that measured me, photographed me, tested me, and sent electronic messages about Professor Rod Damon directly into the complex wiring systems of the giant computers. The computers already possessed my measurements, so that within a certain area of information, they were now ready to accept detailed data.

The relay systems worked steadily. Lights flashed on in banks and in individual parts here and there across the computer-face. I did not see the lights but I heard the faint little clicks as the computers went to work. Those warm rays were taking my blood pressure, my metabolism, my heartbeat. They analyzed my skin, they tested my temperature. They did about everything it might take a hundred highly skilled medical men a year to find out. All in the matter of maybe half an hour.

Somebody began undoing my straps.

Fedor Novotny said, "There we are, Professor. That's all for now. Everything has gone like clockwork."

"That's all there is to it?"

"Not quite all. There still remain some delicate investigations to be made, but these can wait a few days."

I turned to my clothes. Lee Chi was there ahead of me, lifting my shorts and holding them as she sank to her knees. I noticed that she turned away her head when I stuck my legs in the proper holes in my shorts. There was a faint smile on her full red lips as her black eyes took in the size of my manhood as it dangled.

I asked, "Did they measure that too?"

"Oh, yes. It is very important."

She seemed willing to talk, so I went on. "These other tests they will make. What are they like?"

"Oh, running, jumping, hopping, that sort of thing. The ray-probes will record your reactions and these will be used as a gauge to test the finished product. In other words, your duplicates must perform exactly as you do, in order to *be* you."

"As you robots are built to be like the master model of girls like Ip Chung and Kai Lai?"

"Yes. They—we, that is—must perform as the master model performs. Of course, we do not have her exact personality, personalities will be programmed for each robot, for the better ones, anyhow, to make her or him as much like a human being as is possible."

She held my coolie pants. I slipped my legs into them. She drew them up about my lean hips and tied the cord that served as a belt.

"What puzzles me is, how can they get a brain inside the head of these robots? Your brain, for instance. There are ten billion neurons inside the normal human skull. To duplicate this complexity, would require a lot of space, maybe a whole floor of a building like the Empire State in New York."

"Fedor Novotny and Dmitri Kolsikoff are geniuses," stated Lee Chi. "They defected from Russia because they were not allowed to continue their experiments on the manufacture of living flesh and plasma. It is with this living flesh and plasma that the malleable exterior of all us robots are covered.

"This was their major contribution to the robotics project here. They can duplicate all human organisms, but there is no need to do this. Just the exteriors must be lifelike. And, of course, the vaginal passages of the female. The rest of our bodies are filled with wires and electronic relay systems. Our brains are in our torsos, actually."

I had read somewhere that all human knowledge of the past ten thousand years could be put in a six-foot cube. Novotny and Kolsikoff did not have much space in their robot girls, but they did not need that much. Their women were programmed for certain purposes, no more.

Each of their productions, even my own duplicates, would be made for certain tasks. The soldiers would need be programmed only to fight, the workers to hoe or dig or harvest, and so on. They could get miniaturized control units inside humanoid chests for those purposes very easily.

When my jacket was on, I turned back and sought out Fedor Novotny. I wanted to watch the process by which processed data was translated into male androids shaped like me. Novotny was pleasant, but firm.

"Permission must be refused, Professor. Our processes must remain secret. You must enjoy your life here. You have no worries, no responsibilities. You can have all the food you want, all the rice wine you can drink, all the women who catch your eye. What more could a man ask?"

I could have told him, but I grinned like a moron and made myself look happy. A vegetable might have been happy the way he suggested. I could not. I told myself I was going to get the hell out of this place as soon as possible.

I realized I might need help.

My hand caught Lee Chi by her smooth golden hand as we walked down the laboratory corridor side by side. She seemed surprised, and turned her puzzled eyes to mine.

"Don't you robots understand tenderness?"

She flushed and nodded. "Yes, of course. But—"

"Well, I like you. I want to be your friend. If I'm going to stay here forever, and you're to be my hostess, we really should get to know one another very well."

"I have no past," she stated flatly.

"I do, however. I'd like to talk about it."

As a bar against the homesickness that might already be working in my psyche? I did not know, but I found it helped to talk about the little country town where I was born, to tell Lee Chi things that happened at the university, relate my earliest memories. We went to the gallery and walked up and down it, enjoying the cool winds, and all the while I chatted.

When I was done, I saw tears in her eyes.

"Hey," I said in mock alarm. "You don't have to go quite so far. Turn off your programming."

She laughed. "I can't. It's built into me, so that I respond as a human girl would respond."

A shaft of sunlight caught her blue linen coolie jacket, outlining her shapely body through its almost transparent folds. "I wish you were human," I found myself saying wistfully. "I like you a lot. Maybe because you're such a good companion."

Her face lit up with a happy smile. "Thank you. It is a great compliment you pay me." Her fingers squeezed mine. Then she asked, as if the idea had just occurred to her, "Would you care to sunbathe?"

I would, indeed. I felt as if I'd been cooped up in this place forever. To be out in the sun, to feel its rays bathing my skin and turning it a rich brown, would be a little like being free.

Lee Chi laughed and caught my hand and ran with me up the gallery stairs. These stairs extended to the top of the cliffs, where a flagstoned terrace more than a hundred yards square had been built for the compound personnel. There were shuffleboards, tennis courts, volleyball courts. There was also an area covered by fine white sand, where a man could lie down and bask in the rays of old Sol.

Towels were on a rack. Lee Chi snatched two up, tossed one to me, and ran out onto the sand. I followed her a little more discreetly. Lee Chi spread her towel, took mine and laid it out. Then she stood up and unbottoned her jacket.

I don't know why I was surprised at her action, I just was. Naturally you are not going to sunbathe all dressed up. I stared as the buttons fell away and she threw back the flaps.

Her breasts were firm and heavy, jutting proudly with large, dark nipples. Those breasts shook as she wriggled her arms out of her sleeves. Her sly eyes caught me staring at her bouncing globes.

She asked sweetly, "Aren't you going to strip too?"

I stripped. The sun was hot on my bare skin, but the breezes sweeping over the cliff top were cooling. I found my manhood was not bothered by Lee Chi's nudity, even though my eyes appreciated her shapely hips and legs and breasts—in a kind of esthetic sense, that is—and that I could stretch out naked beside her without wanting her body.

After all, she was a robot. My phallus knew it.

I fell asleep for a little while. When I woke up my skin tingled with that familiar bite of sunburn. It felt good, lying here like this. I could forget my worries about escaping. I turned over on my front.

My companion was fast asleep, which surprised me. I was even more surprised to discover that her skin was showing a bit of burn too.

Where her thick black hair grew from her temples, there was a film of sweat. She was feeling the sun's heat just as I was. I marveled at the almost magical qualities of this almost-human flesh which Novotny and Kolsikoff had created.

Then I did a kind of double-take.

Hold on a minute, now. These robots had to be programmed to sweat. They could not do it by themselves, as the human body did. Sweating is a completely reflex action. Nobody ever wills himself to sweat. It happens because of nervous tension or too much heat or humidity.

I got up, I walked all around the flagstoned patio until I found a sharp stone. I brought it back and, lying down, scratched Lee Chi in the wrist.

She woke up, yelping and clamping a hand to herself.

"You damned little liar," I breathed in utter admiration.

"Wha—what?" she gasped.

Her reactions had been fast, but I'd managed to see the tiny drop of blood well up wetly from her cut flesh. I put my lips to her cut, brushing away her hand. I sucked her tiny wound until it did not bleed any more.

Then I lay back and put my hands behind my neck, eyes closed. I said, "They're going to kill me, aren't they?"

"What makes you say that?"

"You're alive, but you pretend to be a robot. Actually

you're the master model for androids like Ip Chung and Kai Lai. Aren't you?"

A soft palm clapped my lips shut. Terrified eyes stared down at me, wide and huge. "Please! Don't even suggest it."

I caught her palm, holding it still as I kissed it. There was the faint taste of sweat on her skin.

"All right," I told her meekly. "I'll keep my voice down. I realize the place may be bugged."

She shook her head, still leaning over me and staring down into my face. Some of her earlier terror was gone from her eyes. She even smiled a little.

"No. It isn't that. I don't mind talking up here. It's when we go down there that makes me worry. If they thought you knew I was real, my life is finished."

Her heavy breasts lay warm on my chest. Their touch stirred the fluttering fires in my loins. My manhood began to take an interest in her as a female.

"That's where the danger is," I rasped, and she followed the direction of my eyes to my slowly rising flesh. "Novotny and the others know I can't function as a man with a female robot—without hypnotism. If they see me like this with you, they'll damn well be suspicious. Be a good girl. Put on some clothes, and take those adorable tits off my chest."

She flushed and giggled, but she did what I said. She kept her back turned as I donned my own coolie wear.

Half in jest, I murmured, "I've always been proud of my erectile powers. Now I'm not so sure. I wouldn't want my phallus to betray your humanity. So I've got to be on my guard all the time."

She said, "Only for about two weeks. That's how long it will take the Russians to complete their tests and to run out perfect duplicates of you, Professor. Then they will kill you dead to make sure you never talk. I'm alive simply because they are sure I'll cooperate and not try to escape."

"I've got to get out of here before then, obviously."

She glanced back at me, eyebrows arched. "How? I wish with all my heart you could—I'd go with you in a flash. But there isn't any way. There just isn't."

"There is. I've got to think of it."

"I'll help you, of course."

"Hmmm. You know the layout here. I don't. You can help

by briefing me as to the exact location of all alarm systems, where the guards hang out, and so on."

She nodded happily. She leaned over and whispered, "I wish I could kiss you, Professor. But I'm afraid of that—that monster of yours."

We went downstairs, where we behaved ourselves circumspectly. Lee Chi showed me around the compound, then brought my evening meal to my round room, where she shared it, pretending to be a robot. Her warning finger lifted to her kissable mouth several times, reminding me that the room was probably bugged.

After dinner we searched the room thoroughly. I finally found the bugging device under a corner of the carpet not far from the big bed. I pointed at it so Lee Chi would know where it was as I said out loud, "It's kind of hot in here. I think I'll move the bed over where the air-conditioner sends down a current of cool air. On second thought, you do it for me, Lee Chi."

I wanted them to think I thought of Lee Chi as a robot. Actually I was the one who stooped and lifted the bed, working it toward the hidden bug. When I had the bed-leg poised over the telltale gadget, I lifted it even higher, then let it go. Its falling weight squashed the listening device absolutely flat.

I grabbed Lee Chi, half dragging her over the headboard, and kissed her thoroughly. Her lips were warm and soft, she was all girl. Real girl. I could feel her nipples getting hard where her breasts mashed my chest through the thin linen of our coolie jackets.

Then I let her go. I didn't want to push it too far, one of the Russians might walk in just when things got interesting. But I did want her to know how I felt about her. She got the message. Her eyes danced; she giggled and then clapped her soft palms over her full lips.

I dragged her down on the bed, but just to talk.

"Tell me all about this place. I saw one of the sailors burn Yi Lou back in Hok Tang. I take it that's the way they get rid of the unwanted robots?"

"They have an incinerator where they burn them. Sometimes, of course, a robot comes all unprogrammed—what you might term 'goes mad.' Then she has to be destroyed before she can hurt anyone."

"How do they do that?"

"The guards have tiny flame-throwers attached to their belts. Their range is not much, about ten feet. But the flames are so hot the robots catch fire and the heat damages their controls immediately so they cannot move. They just stand there and are consumed."

"Those guards—are any of them robots?"

"Oh, yes. The more robots they use, the less people they have to worry about feeding—or talking."

"Is there any way of knowing a robot from a real person?"

She lifted my hand and put it to the back of her neck where I felt the smooth, soft skin and under it the cervical vertibrae. "A robot will have a ceramic plate here," She explained.

I went on stroking her neck. She nuzzled her head into my neck as she rested it on my shoulder. It was more than disturbing to fall asleep with that bundle of golden curves cuddled up to me, but I managed it. Just before I drifted off, I managed to work out a plan of action for our escape. My fingers were crossed on both hands when I started to dream.

Next morning, we acted like robot and master for the whole compound to see. Lee Chi stood behind me as I ate, she brought me coffee and food, she sneaked little bites of food when nobody was looking. Since she was supposed to be with me all the time and robots do not eat, Lee Chi had to grab her vitamins on the gallop, so to speak. She had become quite adept at it.

She helped herself to the vitamin supply the Robot Development Center kept for the human beings. She snitched eggs and ate them raw. She grabbed glasses of milk on their way into the dining hall. She had to be careful so as not to lose weight, and be sure she did not gain weight. It was a problem, all right, but she had managed it so far.

We decided it might be best to make our try to get away at once, without waiting. I put on my happy face when I met Kang Chow, and later when I stopped to chat with Fedor Novotny.

They seemed pleased that I was accepting my new role in life with such good grace. I nodded pleasently to all the personnel we encountered along the corridors.

Lee Chi pinched me as we walked along an empty tunnelway. "There! I know that one. He is a robot."

There was a guard up ahead, standing stiff and straight, staring straight ahead down an intersecting corridor. My heart picked up its beat. I could see the portable flame-thrower attached to his belt. I kept on walking and felt Lee Chi pressing something round and smooth into my palm.

It was a pretty stone paperweight she had stolen from a desk past which we had walked, flat on one side. It would do just as nicely as the leather-covered sap with which Shu Shang had broken the ceramic plete of Yi Lou. My fingers tightened around it.

I started my swing from the floor.

The robot guard was completely unsuspecting.

The paperweight slammed into his ceramic plate with the force of an express train. It made a dull cracking sound when it hit. The robot guard gave off sparks from the opening in his neck-covering, then fell forward.

I grabbed the flame-thrower.

Lee Chi whispered frantically, "We can't leave him here. Somebody might find him. Wait! There are storage closets along these corridors. Over here!"

We dragged the guard along the tunnel. It would have been easier to burn him to ashes, I suppose, but the burning would take a little time and only God knew who might come strolling along here.

I closed the door on the inert thing.

"Professor Damon!" a voice called.

I whirled, feeling my heart sink. The flame-thrower was on the floor near the closet door where I'd set it to open the door. And Dmitri Kolsikoff was hurrying toward me.

"It is time for our love festival, Professor. I am sure you would be interested in seeing it."

I waited, my back to Lee Chi, whom I could hear breathing in nervous gusts behind me. I called, "I'd be delighted, Doctor Kolsikoff. Er—how do I get there?"

"I would go with you, but I am otherwise occupied. Lee Chi will see you safely there. Lee Chi! What are you doing?"

The girl stepped forward. "The storage room door was open, sir. I merely closed it securely."

Kolsikoff nodded, stared hard at us a moment, then turned on a heel and walked away. I turned to stare at the flame-thrower. It was gone.

"I kicked it into the closet," Lee Chi panted, grabbing my arm and hurrying me along. "I had to open and shut the door. Your back was to me, you hid what I was doing from Kolsikoff, but I guess he saw the door moving."

"If they find that robot, we're done for."

She nodded soberly. "I know. You they will keep alive until the final tests are made. Me, I'll die right away."

We walked in gloom all the way to the love festival.

It was held in a large room surrounded by tiered seats such as were in the observation room where I had been hypnotized about Feng Ti. Soft mattresses had been spread all across the floor. A raised mattress stood on a dais in the middle of the room. There was nobody in the seats.

"What do we do?" I asked.

"We sit and watch, I guess. The male personnel are given this love festival every week, to make sure their tensions at this confinement do not build up too much. Instead of the saltpeter they hand out to prisoners in your United States prisons, the Red Chinese use this method."

"I like your way better," I said. As we sat down to await developments, I got an inspiration. "Listen! If all the personnel are in here making love, why don't we just slip out and make our break for it? Everybody will be too busy to notice us."

Lee Chi turned her head, eyes brilliant with hope. "Oh, yes! I should have thought of that myself. It is the one time there won't be any real people in the compound, except for this room. Oh, it's marvelous!"

A blue door opened in the far wall.

About three hundred Chinese dolls came prancing in, wearing their coolie jackets and pants. Each girl went to a mattress and stood there, waiting.

Lee Chi leaned to my ear. "When they were building this place, they employed more than three thousand people. They gave it out that the work they did was to beautify and preserve the Buddhist cave paintings. So nobody is the wiser in Red China, except the higher-ups.

"Today, of course, only about three hundred real people are involved in the running of this place. All of them are male." She giggled. Except me, of course."

The men were filing in now. They were all Chinese, and

they were headed by Kang Chow. The thought touched my mind that under Communism, even their loving was done by herd instinct.

At the rear of the column came the two Russians.

Fedor Novotny had a big grin, indicating the fact that he was already relishing the fun-time ahead. Dmitri Kolsikoff was faintly scowling. The sex drive didn't run so fast in him, I felt. This was almost a chore to the smaller man. He would have been much happier somewhere deep in his laboratories.

Lee Chi slid her hand into mine. Being only human, she slid forward to the edge of her seat and her red tongue ran around her lips. Well, I was almighty curious myself, but my mind was on escape rather than on eroticism.

In short minutes, no matter how interesting things got down there on those mattresses, Lee Chi and I would be on our way. We would grab the flame-thrower, mow down any robot guard that tried to stop us, and be out of this place in minutes—long before they finished the love festival.

I sat back, completely relaxed.

I was as good as on my way to Hong Kong.

Then a voice cut through my dreamings. "Professor Damon!"

It was Kang Chow calling. He stood there beaming his smile up at my astonished face. As a matter of fact they were all looking up at me.

"Will you lead us in love, Professor?"

My heart sank. I heard Lee Chi gasp with the realization that every eye was on us. Escape was impossible, if I had to go down to the one unoccupied mattress and play a frolicking follow-the-leader! My dreams went smash before reality.

I stood up and bowed. "I would be honored, Kang Chow. But as you know, I have a very definite trauma about robot women."

Kang Chow smiled grimly. "Try anyhow, Professor!"

They knew! my thudding heart told me. They realized I knew Lee Chi was human and no android. They had chosen this way to expose us with all the traditional deviousness of the Chinese mind. Dmitri Kolsikoff had seen Lee Chi kick the flame-thrower into the closet and knew we were up to something, but he had remained quiet, knowing what was coming.

Lee Chi cast me a despairing glance as she stood up.

She led the way to the slaughter.

CHAPTER NINE

Lee Chi stood beside the mattress on the raised dais. Her head was high and her full lips smiled, but in the black eyes there was heartbreak and despair which only I could read. She knew as well as I what this meant. I would get erotically excited by her human body. I was not supposed to get excited because I should have believed her to be a robot.

The Red Chinese had thought up a real mean way of making me betray Lee Chi to them. They would torture her to make her tell of our escape plans. No matter how brave she was, the Chinese knew ways to torment the human body that would make a wooden Indian howl.

Kang Chow began speaking.

"We will follow your lead, Professor. What you do with Lee Chi, we shall do with our own love mates. Since you are on the raised dais, it is easy for us to see you both."

Was there a hint of mocking laughter in his voice?

He said, "You are known as a true adept in the love postures. Even in Maoist China, we know of your priapic prowess. We all have yearned to match strokes with you, deep in our hearts. Call it male jealousy if you will—but the need is there.

"Now we are going to get that chance!

"Lay on, Professor!"

The bastard!

I lifted my hands to the wooden buttons on Lee Chi's coolie jacket and undid the first three. Then I dragged the jacket down off her shoulders and to her upper arms. The front of the jacket I then drew together just beneath her jutting breasts. I buttoned the jacket flaps so that they pushed her boldly thrusting breasts upward and forward.

I glanced down at the rest of the gang.

Six hundred golden breasts poked outward above three hundred tightly buttoned coolie jackets. "If this is the way I'm going to go," I thought. "I'll make it a memorable experience!" I leaned and licked Lee Chi across each jutting nipple.

She moaned, unable to stop that sound of utter delight. Her breasts were familiar to me; I had made lip and lingual love to the bosoms of Ip Chung and Kai Lai. I knew their responses, their full curves. After all, Ip Chung and Kai Lai had been made in Lee Chi's shape and form.

My lips gathered in her big nipples, one after the other. Below me, three hundred male heads bent and did what I did. Lee Chi was shifting her rounded hips in her growing need for satisfaction. I could hear her linen trousers scratching together as her thighs worked.

My fingers went under her jacket, carressed her smooth torso flesh, all the way up to the tightened coolie jacket. Then I slid them downward, easing down her elasticized trouser belt, until the coolie pants were caught on the wide sweep of her bared hips.

Over her lower belly and upper buttocks I slid my fingertips gently, like feathers. Lee Chi was gasping in pleasure. So were three hundred other female throats, slightly below us.

I fondled, I teased. Lee Chi was making her hips go back and forth in rut-need. Ditto the three hundred female robots below.

I knelt and slowly, ever so slowly, drew down the coolie pants. I leaned to kiss her undercurve of belly. She let her head fall back and a low wail rose from her corded throat. My lips traced a network of caresses about her upper thighs, her hips. I turned her, devoted my attentions to her quivering buttocks.

I could hear the men now. They were growling, rasping curses. I gathered that I was prolonging connection far too long. I wondered at the intelligence of the other leaders the group might have had. What did they expect me to do, throw her down on the mattress and just hammer away? I wanted Lee Chi to have a good time too.

Even if it was for the last time.

I expected to hear Kang Chow yell up at me, ordering me to hurry it up, but he played the game. He was suffering along with all the rest of the males, but he meant what he said about trying to stay with me.

I teased Lee Chi a little longer about the backs of her

upper thighs before I turned her and lifted her left leg onto my shoulder. Her hands came down to tangle in my hair as my lips kissed and my teeth nibbled her sensitives.

After about ten minutes, she panted, "Please! Oh, please!"

I put her down on the mattress very gently.

Then I squatted in the *lebeuss el djoureb* of the Arabs, in which the slow insertion of the male member is aided by the vaginal flow of the female, and then begins a rhythmic to and fro swaying. This "fitting on the sock" is designed to give the woman the greatest pleasure, but the man enjoys it just as much.

I swung into a side posture, the *djenabi,* with Lee Chi on her side and with yours truly fitted into her, likewise on my side.

As a matter of fact I went through all eleven manners of the Arabs, with Lee Chi flat on her back or on her side, or stretched with her knees wide apart as she knelt in the manner of the cow with the bull.

The hours went by and I went on and on.

Forgotten were the men and robot women below us. Lee Chi was my world, a world of sobs and gritted teeth, of fingernails raking my back, of thighs clamped tight about my middle. She was smooth and soft and perfumed, a mass of erogenous ecstasy. Her head went back and forth or rubbed savagely against the mattress-covering in her uncontrolled convulsions of delight. She was wet with sweat, but the hell with that. Since Kang Chow and the Russians had seen me with my priapus ready for her pleasure, they knew damn well she was not a robot.

Until this moment, I suddenly realized, there had been sounds and screams and curses rising up to my ears. Now I could hear only the harsh pantings of Lee Chi and my own bull-like breathing.

I risked a glance to my side.

The men lay collapsed in the arms and thighs of the robot women. Dmitri Kolsikoff was snoring, Fedor Novotny was smiling blissfully. The Chinese men were equally asleep, worn out with their erotic endeavors.

Hah! I remembered the words of Ip Chung and Kai Lai. So a Red Chinese man would put me to shame in the amative art, would he? Here were hundreds of them scattered about on their love mattresses and they had all caved in long, long ago.

I was still going strong.

I grinned down at Lee Chi. "Come on, honey—let's beat feet. There's nobody around to stop us."

Her arms and thighs tightened about me. "More," she breathed. "Oh, more! I've never known anything like this. Please, please."

Jeez! No wonder Ip Chung and Kai Lai had been such heterocoital hounds! Lee Chi was the master model.

So I devoted myself to her.

I went through three of the erotic exploits of the legendary hero Kokah Pundit, by which he hoped to overcome the priestess demon Naugee-Devah, before Lee Chi fainted. She was what Naugee-Devah had been, a *jigger-khweyyah* or one-who-eats-the-liver-of-a-man, with her amorous embraces. Any normal male would have given up long ago, with Lee Chi. Me, I was just warming up.

I got to my feet. I bent and picked Lee Chi up in my arms. I walked down the few steps of the dais and stepped a path between the mattresses. I was going to walk out of this place with her and nobody was going to stop me. Or so I thought.

But at this moment—

Dmitri Kolsikoff got to his knees, then rose to his feet at sight of me. He was scowling malignantly.

"Go to your room, Professor. Fedor and I must consult about you. Guards! Guards!"

Our escape plans went flying in the running feet of the guards who came racing into the rooms to take up their position on either side of me. Kolsikoff nodded his head.

"Food will be brought to you, Professor," he snapped.

I stared back at him. "Am I a prisoner?"

His shoulders shrugged. "Perhaps, perhaps not. It is what I wish to consult about." His eyes touched Lee Chi, who lay there in my arms dead to the world. "And about that one, as well."

The fat was in the fire. I carried Lee Chi back to my round room and put her down on the bed. Dmitri Kolsikoff knew Lee Chi was human, and suspected that she and I were working in cahoots to escape.

The delegation came three hours later. It consisted of

Kang Chow and the two Russians. Kang Chow was beaming in delight, so was Fedor Novotny. Only Dmitri Kolsikoff was frowning.

With both hands, Kang Chow caught my right hand, shaking it. "Professor, never has there been such a love festival as there was today. It lasted close to four hours! Everyone agrees that as a love leader, you are a veritable Shou Lou. My congratulations!"

I was flabbergasted. I looked at Fedor Novotny.

"I thought at first I was going to fail you," I told him. "You see, with a robot woman such as Lee Chi—"

Novotny clapped me on the shoulder with a hamlike hand. His laughter boomed out and bounced around from wall to wall.

"Professor, I hypnotized you. Remember? You see robot women as real women now. And you always will."

Kolsikoff snarled. "I do not like it, I tell you. This man is a monster! He will kill everyone by making them love themselves to death trying to keep up with him."

Novotny gave his friend a good-natured push. "Go on, Dmitri. Just because you are undersexed, don't try to spoil things for the rest of us. No, no. Kang Chow and I have voted him perpetual love leader and that is how it shall be. Imagine sharing the erotic knowledge and know-how of Professor Rod Damon!"

I said, "I'm flattered, naturally. But I had hoped to go back to the university and—"

Kang Chow held up a hand. "I am sorry, Professor. But that cannot be. You see, we had intended to kill you after we completed our final tests. Your performance today was so marvelous that we voted against that drastic measure. Instead, you will live on, closely guarded, to lead us in our revels every week!"

"Closely guarded?" I echoed weakly.

"Professor! Do you realize how many robot women saw you in action today? Remember, they have been programmed to make love, to lust for love as a method of learning state secrets, when we are ready to turn them loose on decadent capitalistic diplomats.

"They will be trying to break down your door to get at you. That is why I must station guards to protect you. You understand, of course?"

I just gawked at him.

His eyes touched Lee Chi and hardened. "As for this one, she must be destroyed. She actually fainted before you were done with her. She didn't even last five hours. Girls like Ip Chung and Kai Lai can go on indefinitely." He was telling me! "Yes, we must destroy her, she is a weakling."

I drew a deep breath. "I find her very pleasing. She makes a good companion. She is always eager to serve me. I would appreciate your making an exception in her case. Let her live to wait on me the way she has been doing."

Kang Chow hesitated. I added the final convincer. "After all, since she is such a lousy lover-girl, she won't sap my strength."

Fedor Novotny grinned. "He has a point there, Chief."

I could hear Lee Chi breathing angrily behind me. I had to put her down a little, but it was only to save her life. I hoped she would understand.

Kang Chow shrugged. "She can exist for a while, until we see how things turn out. But no other robot women are to see you." He swung on Lee Chi. "Do you understand me, Lee Chi? You have not been programmed to be jealous, but you are programmed to protect. You shall protect Professor Damon from any other woman, real or robotic."

"I understand, Professor," she said.

When the door closed on our visitors, she aimed a palm at my face. I ducked and grabbed her arms. She was flushed with rage and insulted femininity.

"Did you have to add that bit about my not being able to weaken you? Did you? Did you? Just because you're some sort of fluttering freak doesn't mean——"

I closed her mouth with a kiss. She moaned and tried to break free but my lips and darting tongue made her remember the pleasures I had given her on the love festival mattress. Her belly slumped into me and she clung tighter.

"I was only saying it to save your life!" I yelled.

"I know, I know you were. I'm just a bitch!"

"Ssssh, ssshhh," I ssshed, wondering if the room was bugged.

We hunted, but found nothing outside the broken bug under the bed. We sat down on the edge of the bed and made plans. The fact that we were going to be guarded all the time didn't add to our ability to escape. One thing we had going for us. I was going to be allowed to live. This meant there was no special hurry to get away.

For four days, Lee Chi and I led a pleasant, lazy life. We sunbathed. We ate well. We explored the corridors of the Buddhist caves, both the reprocessed ones and the old. We even found a new cave with beautiful paintings in it. If I'd been an archeologist, I would have been thrilled to death.

Actually I went to Kang Chow all excited by my find. I told him about the wall paintings and asked permission to photograph them for the state. He was delighted at my cooperation. He would furnish all the cameras and films I would need. I said nothing about the guards who had accompanied Lee Chi and me to the painted caves. I figured Kang Chow would think of them himself.

Next morning when we went out, the guards lazed on benches before the door of my round room. They smiled and shook their heads when I asked if they were coming along.

"There is no need, Professor. No robot women are allowed in the unexplored sections of the caverns."

I said, "Well, you know best."

Lee Chi and I ran for the corridor closet where we'd pushed the broken robot. It was probably asking too much to find the robot and the flame-thrower still in the closet, but I was amazed it hadn't been found yet. When Lee Chi opened the closet door, there they were.

I grabbed the flame-thrower, turned it on the robot. It made a satisfying mass of flames as I left it in the closet with the door open to create a draft. The closet was wood. So were the walls of the corridors. Before we were a hundred yards away, we could hear those flames eating their way through this corner of the Robot Development Center.

We ran on, into the office. A robot woman saw us. The flame-thrower took care of her. In seconds the whole office was on fire. I threw open the control system panel, baring the intricate wires inside. I lifted the flame-thrower and gave it a shot of blaze. The wires curled up and died.

Then we were out on the gallery floor and Lee Chi was whirling toward the emergency switch. She threw it down. I watched the steel grilles drop into place over every cave-mouth opening in the cliffs. The robot women, robot guards and all the personnel of Robot Development Center were penned inside their burning tunnels.

We could hear the fire-alarm bells clanging as we ran down the wooden staircase to the ground. I imagined how the living personnel must be running around inside the Robot Development Center trying to fight those flames. They would not realize they had been trapped inside the caves; not yet, at least. Only when they tried to escape would they find the steel grilles down and locked in place.

I had destroyed their only way of lifting the bars.

Well, that was how the fortune cookie flaked.

If they could stop the flames, they would live. If not—I told myself it was dog eat dog, in the secret agent game. The Red Chinese were out to kill everybody who wasn't with them. I was stopping them by locking them inside the blazing inferno that was the caves.

I got in the black Daimler. Lee Chi slid into the suicide seat beside me. I started the engine, and noticed that the gas tank was at full. I backed up. Now we could hear the roar of the flames and the screams of the men trapped inside them. The thought occurred to me that as soon as the heat reached a certain degree, the highly flammable bodies of the robots would catch fire and add their heat to the conflagration.

My foot shoved down the accelerator.

The Daimler roared off in a cloud of dust.

Lee Chi was clasping her knees with her arms, huddled in the seat beside me. She was damn near bursting with excitement and hope. Once she asked, "Do you think we'll make it? Do you?"

"I'm still dressed like a Chinaman. We've got a chance."

I was reckoning without the radios in the Robot Development Center. When Kang Chow saw that they were trapped in the hell of flames, he must have radioed the authorities, explaining what had happened. This is the way I reconstructed it, because after we had gone about eighty miles, we saw a Chinese army helicopter moving across the horizon.

Its driver had seen us, and angled its course to intercept us at a roadway junction. I saw a machine gun barrel slide out a door where a soldier sat ready to kill us.

My hands on the steering wheel laid out a zigzag pattern on the road. The machine gun spat lead at us, and I saw the marks of the bullets in the dirt of the road as they made tiny dust geysers all around us. We were flirting with death every second, with the odds against us.

Ahead of us I saw water, the river down which the *Pai Lu* had come from Hong Kong. I drove straight for the water.

"Get ready to jump!"

Lee Chi was sobbing in mingled fright and excitement. She put her hand on the door-handle and turned her head to watch me. I left the road, hurling the car under some trees, figuring the leafy branches would hide us for a little while.

The machine gun spat lead at the trees. A couple of spent bullets hit the Daimler and ricocheted off its black surface. I braked the car to a stop. Overhead, the helicopter was whirly-blading off to one side, about to sweep down on us again.

My hand pushed Lee Chi. "Out!" I yelled.

We ran below the trees for about two hundred yards. The river lay before us, cool and inviting. We had to wait, though, until the helicopter was finishing its run. Otherwise, we would be seen and the men in the helicopter would know we were in the river.

Then a river patrol boat would pick us up.

The chopper craft made another swing over the woods. The man with the machine gun must have figured out just about where the car was, from the sound of the ricocheting bullets, if he could hear them pinging over the roar of the whirlybird motor.

His second burst of bullets zeroed in neatly on the Daimler, they rained off the roof and the hood. Then the helicopter was above us and moving forward to begin its swing back. I figured the gunner was having himself a ball, shooting sitting ducks in that car.

I got a better idea.

Bent over, I ran back toward the car. Out of the tonneau I yanked the portable flame-thrower where I'd left it. I got down, hunching myself against the rain of bullets that were coming.

This was madness, but my brain told me it was the only way. When the chopper craft came overhead and the machine-gunner laid his pattern at the Daimler, I was going to give him a helping hand.

I waited, hardly breathing.

The whirlybird swooshed off to the north and west, then

came looping around in a big curve, its blades rotating like crazy. Through the spaces between the leaves I could make out the gunner hanging out his door. The barrel tilted my way.

Bullets rained down on the car, playing out a rat-a-tat-tat on metal. I held my breath, expecting to absorb hot lead myself. My finger hit the controls of the flame-thrower.

Red fire enveloped the car.

I whirled and ran.

The explosion as the gas tank went up caught me fifty feet away. I was picked up and hurled bodily through the air, to land with a thud on forest grass. I rolled over and over. My coolie jacket on fire.

The flames were searing my flesh. They hurt like holy hell. I bit my lip against the pain and fought the jacket to get it off. Then hands touched me, ripping and tearing.

Lee Chi tossed the blazing jacket on the ground. "Stamp on it!" I ordered. "They mustn't see any flames so far away from the car."

She did what I said with her slippered feet.

The helicopter moved away from the sky. It came back to swoop low. The driver and the machine-gunner must see all those flames. They would think we were inside the car, burning to death. In their minds it would be a just retribution, since we had set fire to the Robot Development Center.

I watched the chopper craft slide away through the sky to the south, probably to make its report. Then I caught Lee Chi by the hand.

We ran for the river. We dove in.

Underwater, we swam as far as we could, then we dared to lift our heads and look around us. The river current was gentle but steady, and most important of all, it was going our way.

We swam. I wanted to put as much distance between the burned-out Daimler and ourselves as I could. I knew damn well that when the Red Chinese sent soldiers, the soldiers would find our tracks leading into the water.

By that time, I hoped to be long gone.

Swimming would not do it. We needed a craft of some sort. We kept our eyes open as we swam, hunting the river-bank for a raft or a boat. No luck. It came dusk and we were still swimming with the current without a boat.

By night, I figured we could travel by land.

We got out of the water. It was almost freezing in our wet garments—I still had my coolie pants, while Lee Chi wore both pants and jacket—so we stripped naked and trudged along that way, holding our clothes over our arms to help them dry.

When Lee Chi stumbled and almost fell, I called a halt. It was well past midnight. We would sleep the rest of the night and travel by daylight. When I told her that, she just sank down and lay there. I followed suit.

Next morning we were up at dawn and walking. We put our dried clothes on, so that we might look to be a Chinaman and his wife out for a stroll. The ordinary peasant might take us for that, but I was positive a soldier would stop us and ask questions.

Toward noon, I halted. My hand caught Lee Chi, dragged her under a bush. My head nodded toward the river.

A brown motorboat was pulled in to the bank. Half a dozen men in the quilt-jacketed uniforms of the Red Chinese soldier clambered out of the boat and set off at a trot along the road. Lee Chi and I shrank down deeper into the bush. We held our breaths. I was positive we had been spotted.

The soldiers ran past our hiding place.

I waited, then looked. One soldier remained seated, beside the boat, dozing. I drew Lee Chi toward me, whispering what I wanted her to do. Me, I slithered through the tall grasses at the river's edge and let myself down gently into the water, with hardly a single ripple. I swam underwater toward the boat.

When I poked my head up, I saw Lee Chi standing in front of the soldier, unbottoning her jacket and showing him her big, heavy breasts.

"This is where I wash my clothes," she was saying.

The soldier was standing, his automatic rifle forgotten, his eyes bulging as they took in the swaying, jerking breasts while Lee Chi got out of her coolie jacket.

She pouted, "I usually wash right where your boat is. Can you move it?"

He shook his head violently, jabbering at her in Chinese so fast I could not make it out. By this time I was rising from the water, moving forward steadily, slowly.

My hand went out toward the AK-47.

Lee Chi put her arms above her head, making her breasts rise up and point their dark nipples at the man. He was goggling at them. He would not have turned away if Mao Tse-tung had called him. He acted as if they were the first female breasts he had even seen.

The rifle was in my hand. I lifted it, put both hands to it, stock and barrel, and drove the butt-plate at the back of his skull. I connected with a sodden *thunk!*

His knees bent. He went down knees-first, hit the ground and rolled over, looking as if he were dead. I motioned Lee Chi to get into the boat. Then I pushed it out into the river.

The engine started smoothly.

I steered the boat downriver and gradually picked up speed. Lee Chi crouched with the AK-47 in her hands. Our eyes were locked on the river waters up ahead of us, as I gunned the boat to full speed. The boat would run out of fuel long before we reached Hong Kong. I knew that. But I also knew that we had to trust to luck and keep going until we were as far from the Robot Development Center as we could get.

We ran all day and then all night, taking turns staying awake. To my delight, I'd found extra cans of gasoline in the forward hold. We used up all the cans by the second day, but we must have put a couple hundred miles between us and the burned-out Daimler.

I was hoping that nobody this far downriver would have heard of what had happened to Kang Chow and the others. I was damned surprised that the helicopter hadn't returned, to tell the truth.

The motorboat conked out about ten in the morning. There was no more gasoline anywhere. We let the current carry us for a time, then I realized I had to sink the boat. If we stayed in it, we would be spotted sooner or later. Our luck had been holding good so far. The main reason for this, I honestly believe, was that the villagers living on the riverbanks recognized the boat as army property and the Chinese peasantry was none too friendly with the men in the khaki quilt jackets.

They had learned long ago to mind their own business where the Red Chinese Army was concerned. They minded their business now. It was no affair of theirs if two non-army people wanted to go take a joy-ride in an army boat. They may even have cheered us on, for all I know.

I sank the boat about noon, listening to the gurgle of the river water as it filled the boat, causing it to settle downward gently. Lee Chi and I swam for the shore.

We found a sunny spot hidden by some bushes and stripped down. We spread our clothes to dry. We were damn hungry, both of us. The boat had no food provisions for the soldiers who had been in it; maybe they were expected to live off the land, which meant robbing the peasants.

Where it came to eating and being seen and maybe caught, or not eating and staying free, we made the right decision. We patted our shrunken bellies and smiled at each other.

We slept in the warm sunlight.

In the dusk of evening we put our dry clothes on and started hiking along the riverbanks. I calculated that roughly speaking we had about three hundred miles to walk. Honestly I never really expected to get out of Red China, but I was going to make the attempt.

Sometime in the middle of the night, Lee Chi and I smelled food. Our dry mouths puckered up, I felt a pain in my middle. The hell with consequences, I told myself. We needed food. We could go no farther without it.

I still had the AK-47. If need be, I would use it to steal that food. Side by side, we tiptoed forward, until we were on the outskirts of a large garden. There were peach trees growing here and plum trees, and even some ling-chih fungus. I gaped, honestly amazed.

It was the first time I had ever seen a Chinese love garden. The peach tree, the plum blossoms, the fungus, all were symbols of the yang and yin principle. Twin shrines had been set up at opposite ends of the garden, one holding a statute of Shou Lou, the other of his female counterpart, Hsi Wang Mu.

I wished I had a camera. But the flashbulb going off would have alerted the owners of the house that their garden was being invaded because hot food offerings had been placed on little tables before each shrine. I had to be satisfied with memorizing the layout of the garden and studying the figures of the two deities so I could duplicate this garden in that wing of the university museum where I placed the collection of erotica I gathered from all corners of the world for my League of Sexual Dynamics.

Lee Chi crouched before the jade statue of Hsi Wang Mu, eating the food placed on the porcelain plates. I devoured the sweet and sour pork and the egg rolls put before Shou Lou. We swallowed the rice wine and drank the little bowls of water.

I waved a hand at big-headed old Shou Lou as I climbed over the stone fence. "Thanks, old-timer," I called softly, and turned to find a giggling Lee Chi close behind me.

"That was a funny place," she laughed.

I told her it was a love garden. I explained that in the old days, before the coming to power of Mao Tse-tung, the Chinese had built love gardens and pavilions as adjuncts to their homes, to exhort their deities for much love and long life. The peach tree, the plum tree, the banana tree, symbolic of earthly lusts, were all a necessary part of them.

The custom was fading out. The modern Chinaman had no time for such conceits; he was too busy parading for Mao Tse-tung. I called down blessings on the heads of that house, which thought so much of the love between man and woman that they erected shrines to it.

"A sad loss," I said, and meant it.

I am no flower child but I do think the world would be a better place if there were more love and less hate and criticism in it. Lee Chi listened to me and my opinions, her eyes wide and earnest, as we walked along through the Chinese moonlight.

"If I ever get out of this and have my own love garden, Professor," she told me in her melodious voice, "I shall put a statute of you in it and offer food to you every night."

I grinned and hugged her as we walked.

We followed the winding Canton river, because it was as good as a compass. It would lead us to Hong Kong. It did not guarantee our safe arrival, but nothing and nobody could do that.

It was close to dawn when we tired.

Lee Chi was yawning, stumbling along with bleary eyes. I studied the few houses past which we walked, the bushes and the trees. If I could find a nice hiding place we would hole up and sleep, then walk through the night again.

The night would be our safest time for travel. There

would be fewer eyes to see us. I finally settled on a little clearing between a lot of tall cattails by the river's edge. I turned and caught Lee Chi by the wrist and drew her with me toward the circle of bare dirt.

We lay down and slept.

A booted toe kicked me awake. I sat up to stare into the flat face of a grinning soldier who had his AK-47 aimed at my bellybutton. Another soldier was yanking Lee Chi upright with a hand fastened in her long black hair.

"Up," said my soldier. "Up!"

I upped to my feet. His rifle barrel signaled me to raise my arms. I lifted them high. Lee Chi was standing with bowed head, the tears running down her cheeks and dropping onto her torn coolie jacket.

We were finished.

CHAPTER TEN

At the business ends of two AK-47s, we were marched out onto a dusty road, and along a stand of chestnut trees. I expected a burst of machine gun fire in my back at any moment, but we just plodded on and on until I saw a big brown helicopter perched on its tires in a field.

This was not the same chopper that had fired on the Daimler. It was a larger version that could hold about a dozen soldiers. As we approached, I saw three more soldiers and the whirlybird pilot emerge from the helicopter.

We walked straight ahead.

Behind us, I heard a burst of automatic rifle fire. I almost fell down dead, figuring the two men behind us were polishing us off. The bullets never thudded into Lee Chi and me.

Instead, I saw the man who'd just come out of the helicopter unslinging their AK-47s, getting ready to go into action. I grabbed Lee Chi, knocked her down, and leaped for the two dead soldiers.

My hands closed on one of the rifles.

I swiveled around and lifted the AK-47. Behind me from the dusty road, that automatic rifle opened up again. Whoever was holding it was a lousy shot, the bullets skipped and danced all around the soldiers in front of the helicopter without hitting them. The men in the Red Chinese quilted jackets were ready to let go with their own artillery when I raised my stolen AK-47.

We Coxemen are trained to fire all kinds of weapons—accurately. I had used an AK-47, that imitation of the Russian AK-50, on the firing range at Foundation Field Headquarters. I had scored perfect scores with it, in practice.

In actual combat conditions I scored another perfect score. My bullets chopped a bloody line across the chests of the soldiers. Blood came out on their quilted jackets as they stood there, gaping at me, their own automatic rifles sagging in their hands.

Their knees sagged. Their bodies tilted slowly, their legs going rubbery under them. They fell.

The pilot was yanking a revolver from his holster. I swung the automatic rifle his way and squeezed off a burst of bullets. Every one cut into him. He stood there dead on his booted feet, eyes wide and staring. He went back on his heels, slammed into the chopper craft and slid groundward.

I whirled, wanting a look at my rescuer.

"Come on out," I yelled. "We're friends!"

The bushes moved. A white woman stepped into view, wearing a torn skirt that had been ripped off just below her behind, and without much more in front. Above her skirt she wore a black brassiere that tried valiantly to hold in her loosely shaking breasts.

Her legs were bare, and there were peasant sandals on her feet. She came toward me with the AK-47 ready in her hands. Her face was dirty, there were dark smudges on her cheeks and jaw, but her black eyes were bright with relief.

When she got a little closer, her eyes got real big.

"Why, Professor! Fancy meeting you here."

Her laughter rang out. She tossed back her head, still advancing toward me on those handsome legs. Her hair was black, faintly streaked with gray. I should have known her, but I didn't.

Not until she got up real close.

"Priscilla Saunders!" I howled.

I ran to her, I threw both arms around her and gave her a great big kiss. She met my mouth with open lips and her tongue drove into my mouth. She rocked me back on my heels with the ardor of her embrace. This hungry wanton was not the Priscilla Saunders I had known!

She felt my priapic response rising against her upper thighs. She wriggled them against me and then pushed free, laughing.

"I'm a widow now, Professor. My husband died almost six months ago. That's why the Red Chinese tried to steal those scrolls from me in Tokyo and Hong Kong. They couldn't carry out their part of the bargain."

"It's a marvel to me you're still alive," I said wryly.

"And to me, too."

"You can tell me about it later. Right now we've got to get the hell out of here."

Lee Chi was at my elbow, staring daggerblades at Priscilla. I caught her by a hand, brought her forward and introduced them. Priscilla smiled and held out her hand. Lee Chi smiled suddenly, to my surprise, and held out her own hand.

The girls were good friends from that moment on.

I took them at a run for the helicopter.

Priscilla asked, "Can you fly that thing?"

"I can and will, as soon as we're aboard. Now into the cabin, both of you."

As Lee Chi put a foot into the cabin, with me below her pushing her upward with both hands on her behind, I got a fast idea. Not pushing Lee Chi, just holding her suspended between helicopter and ground, I looked at the widow.

"What about your scrolls, honey?" I asked.

"The Red Chinese have them."

"Yeah, I figured that. But where?"

Her arm lifted. Her finger pointed at the village I had seen in the distance. "There. I got away at dawn and hid. The villagers alerted the army, I guess, because the helicopter came when I was hiding in those big bushes beside the road.

"I watched them searching the entire area. I had stolen a rifle from my guard whom I hit over the head with a rock. I was going to sell my life dearly when they found me. Instead, they brought you in."

So much for vanity. I'd figured the helicopter and all these soldiers were here because of Lee Chi and me. It had been pure dumb luck that they'd found us piling up the zzzs.

I looked across the fields at the village. The Chao Meng Fu scrolls were about a mile away. All the instincts of the treasure hunter, the bandits of history, the gold seekers and the greedy-guts of all Time, churned in my middle.

It wasn't for their value that I wanted those scrolls: not for the money I could get for them, that is. I wanted those Chao Meng Fu masterpieces for the Eros wing of the university museum. They would be the star attraction of the League for Sexual Dynamics exhibits.

My fingers tightened on my AK-47 rifle. "Take me there," I told Priscilla.

Her face went ashen. "They'll kill us!"

"Who? A lot of villagers? We're armed, they won't dare try to stop us."

Lee Chi wriggled her backside, saying, "Let me down. I can handle an automatic rifle. All us Chinese girls are taught to fight."

She sounded very proud of the fact, so I let her down gently to the ground. She ran to the nearest dead body and snatched up the fallen weapon.

Then we set off across the fields, using the bushes and trees as shelter. As we moved along, Priscilla Saunders talked.

"They keep the scrolls in the largest hut, that's a sort of communal meeting house. There are two old men there—scholars, both of them—who came to identify the scrolls as the authentic work of Chao Meng Fu. I guess they didn't trust the judgment of Pak Dong."

"What about soldiers?"

"Outside of the one guard I slugged, there aren't any—but there are a number of young Red Guards in the village. They've been stationed there to give the peasants a hand with the crops. They may fight."

We moved forward slowly. Most of the people in the town were out in the fields, planting or harvesting or some damn thing. I figured we were playing in real luck. Our feet skirted the back of the huts on our side of the one road. When we were behind the largest hut, we stepped forward.

My hand lifted a bamboo screen.

Two old men were bent over a table, rolling up the scrolls inside a glossy, imitation leather carrying case. The guard was watching them, his head bandaged. Two tough-looking young teenagers—Red Guards, I was positive—stood at the doorway, framing it with their bodies and looking out across the fields.

If they had heard the sound of gunfire, they must have

assumed that the soldiers had found Priscilla Saunders, that she had put up some kind of struggle, and that she was now dead.

"Hold it right where you are!" I snapped.

The Red Guards whirled. The soldier looked up. The two old men went on sliding the scrolls into the leather case. I waited until they fastened the straps that held it.

"You—back up!" I ordered the soldiers.

One of the Red Guards turned on a heel and ran out the door. He took me completely by surprise. Not so with Lee Chi. Her barrel spat red flame. The youth arched his back and went down the steps in a flying stumble. I saw the pattern of red on his back that showed where Lee Chi had pumped a dozen bullets into him.

The soldier moved back half a dozen steps.

I motioned to Priscilla to get the scrolls. She stepped forward, hand outstretched. One of the old men lifted his right hand and leaped for her. A dagger glinted in his wrinkled hand. Priscilla was between us. I couldn't fire, neither could Lee Chi.

Priscilla said, "Haaa!"

Her two hands grabbed the thin old wrist, bent it sideways. The other old man leaped for her.

I jumped forward.

While Priscilla struggled with her attacker, my riflebutt drove over her head into the face of the old man who was coming to lend his help. I sympathized with them. I knew how valuable and how rare those scrolls were. But I wanted them for me.

The man I hit went backward, nose smashed. I turned to help Priscilla but the soldier and the Red Guard were getting in on the action too. They dove for me, the soldier yanking out a revolver, the Red Guard a long knife.

It was too close to use the AK-47. I couldn't even swing it. I fell forward, half throwing myself at the knees of the soldier. He hit me and toppled, just as a would-be tackler might be taken out of the play by a veteran blocking back. I was on my knees. I whirled for the Red Guard who was aiming his knife at me.

My hands caught him, swung him sideways.

Lee Chi was crouched behind us, rifle barrel up. As the

Red Guard hurtled away from me, she squeezed her trigger and damn near cut him in half with her spray of bullets.

The old man struggling with Priscilla Saunders cried out in a high, shrill voice. My eyes darted his way. The widow had turned his wrist, had driven the long knife-blade into his belly. The old man tottered, fell against the table and collapsed half over it before he dropped to the floor.

Priscilla grabbed the leather carrying case.

I landed with both knees on the soldier. The breath whooshed out of him as his front slammed into the flooring. My hands raised the AK-47. I drove its butt plate downward.

When the soldier came to, he was going to have a headache to end all headaches. I got up, seeing Lee Chi and Priscilla waiting for me at the bamboo curtain that Lee Chi was holding up.

"Go on," I yelled. "I'm coming."

We ran like crazy across the fields. Behind us we could hear the angry cries and screeches of the villagers, aroused by the sound of gunfire in their own huts. Some of them carried pitchforks, some held hoes. There were half a dozen Red Guards with them, easily out-distancing the older men.

I boosted Lee Chi up into the whirlybird. Priscilla was dancing around in her eagerness. She tossed the scrolls up to Lee Chi, put a sandaled foot on my thigh and let me shove her upward.

I whirled. I aimed the AK-47 in the general direction of the oncoming villagers and gave them a fast burst. Two of the foremost Red Guards went down. The others slowed their run, and fell flat.

I tossed the automatic rifle up into the chopper craft and went after it. Priscilla was there to lend a hand. Lee Chi crouched at an open door, her own weapon ready to fire.

I leaped for the pilot's seat.

The motor started and revved up smoothly. Overhead, the blades sliced the air with a clean stroke, building speed. I handled the controls with a little unfamiliarity, this Red Chinese copter was only vaguely similar to the one I'd learned to fly at the Thaddeus X. Coxe Foundation training center, but I got it up into the air.

I checked the compass.

Then I made a wide swing about five hundred feet up in the

air and headed for Hong Kong. Priscilla sagged down behind me while Lee Chi sank back into her seat.

"We're on our way," I yelled.

The girls were quiet for about fifteen minutes. Priscilla Saunders had stationed herself half over my right shoulder so that if I glanced away from the control board, I would be sure to see her big white breasts in their cobwebby black brassiere. When she exhaled, the breasts seemed to shrink slightly in the black nylon cups so I could catch a glimpse of her brown nipples.

When she drew in breath, the breasts ballooned outward, bulging above the bra cups. It was very intriguing. I saw that Lee Chi was smiling faintly, watching the direction of my eyes.

"You are good friends, you two?" she asked.

Priscilla would have blushed, some days ago. Now she put her bare left arm about my neck and hugged me. "We ought to be what you call 'good friends.' Unfortunately, we are only acquaintances. Traveling companions."

She went on to tell her story to a sympathetic Lee Chi. The Chinese girl was very interested. Her lips were partly open and her eyes sparkled as Priscilla explained how she and I had become excited in the Tokyo coffee shop and how she had gone off all by her lonesome, working her hips against mine.

And how later, in the Tokyo hotel, she would not let me take her. Lee Chi tch-tched and shook her head at the unwisdom of Caucasian females.

"I was a married woman," exclaimed Priscilla hotly.

"Now you are a widow. You see how wrong it is to keep the door locked when opportunity knocks?"

Priscilla smiled faintly, and let her brassiered breasts stir against my neck. Her breasts seemed to be getting bigger, or else the bra cups were shrinking. They wobbled and trembled almost out of the sheer nylon.

"Suppose we hadn't happened along and those soldiers had found you? They'd have killed you and you'd have gone to the grave without knowing the joy of Rod Damon's rod."

Priscilla looked slightly stunned. "You mean, you've sampled it?"

"Oh my, yes. Shall I tell you?"

"Please do," muttered Priscilla coldly.

Lee Chi told about how I had been invited into Red China to have robot males made from my body. Of course, now that we had left the Robot Development Center a blazing inferno, no machines could have come through that holocaust unscathed, so there would be no more robots, either male or female.

The personnel, including the two Russians and their inventions, would all perish. Red China would have to depend on its depleted manpower now, without android help. I had found out about the robots and destroyed them—while servicing Lee Chi.

She told how my body would not respond to Feng Ti without hypnosis. Then she giggled, "But you should have seen him in action after Fedor Novotny worked on his psyche with his watch."

"I'd have loved to," breathed Priscilla Saunders. She sounded as if she might be thawing.

"Maybe I can describe it," exclaimed Lee Chi cheerfully.

She was a regular Michelangelo with words, this pretty Chinese doll. She told how Feng Ti and I had made it together until they had to pull us apart with a dozen or more hands and then stick me with a hypodermic needle to bring down my manhood.

"My goodness!" cried the widow, eyeing me with bold black eyes. Her breasts rubbed harder against the back of my neck.

Lee Chi told about how she and I had played love-in follow-the-leader for the personnel at the Robot Development Center. In detail and highly colored by admiration for my manly qualities.

I flushed with embarrassment, and maybe something else, because Lee Chi leaned over and put her hand down on me, gently stroking the stiffness of my everready phallus that had been enlivened by her talk and the feel of the Saunders breasts.

"I'll bet a fortune cookie you don't believe me," Lee Chi said to Priscilla.

The two girls exchanged a meaning glance.

Priscilla said, "I certainly do not. I ought to have some proof."

A hand slid my zipper down.

I said, "Hold everything—no, wait! Not quite that way."

Too late. Lee Chi had hold of me and Priscilla was staring with bulging eyes and drooping lips. She was starting to breathe faster, which was why her mouth was open.

"Priscilla," I protested. "Remember your puritanical upbringing. You really shouldn't—"

"I psyched myself, Professor—like it says in your book. Oh, yes. I bought a copy of *The Sex Machine* in Hong Kong and read it on my way into the interior. You are a genius, Professor. Your theory really works."

Priscilla leaned forward and removed Lee Chi's hand, substituting her own. Her fingers were cool and smooth. My hips bucked.

"If you think I can steer a course to Hong Kong while you're feeling around—"

Lee Chi ignored me to ask Priscilla, "You really mean it when you say you have not had a man in more than a year?"

"I really do, honey."

"Shame on you, Professor. You should never have let her plead her way out of bedding down with you in that Tokyo hotel room." Then Lee Chi nudged me with her elbow. "Out, out. I can fly this whirlybird too, Let me demonstrate."

"You doll," breathed the widow.

Lee Chi chuckled. "First grabs to you, Priscilla. Then I'll think of a way to get my own licks in."

"Will there be anything left? I mean . . . . "

"Show her, Professor!" shouted Lee Chi.

I got into a back seat. I would have used a little foreplay—it is always a good idea to rouse up a woman before you take her, as I have taught again and again in my courses in the League for Sexual Dynamics—but there was no need for this with the widow lady. She was already "bursting her cloud" at the mere idea of joining her body with mine.

Priscilla Saunders simply lifted her torn skirt, under which she was naked, and put her left leg over my lap, straddling my thighs. She sat down slowly, with quite evident relish, judging by the little cries of ecstasy she emitted. She put her arms about me and held me to her open-mouthed kiss while her hips fandangoed all over me.

Up and down and sideways went her hips. I marveled at her virtuosity, considering her background.

When I mentioned it, she panted, "I've kept myself in check all my life, Professor. First, because I thought it was my duty to come to my marriage bed a virgin. Then when I was a married woman, I felt it was my duty to be faithful to Martin. Even if he was in China.

"Now I'm going to make up for it."

There was no sense in sitting here like a bump on a log, letting her do all the work. I ran my fingers up her bare thighs to her belly and around it to her sides and upward, pushing her skirt to her armpits. My fingers hooked her thin brassiere and tugged it down so that the crumpled cups held her big breasts pushed out.

Between forefingers and thumbs, I grabbed her nipples. I rotated them; I pulled them. She sobbed in heat as my tongue licked and my mouth opened to nurse. My hands went down to her buttocks.

She tore off her skirt over her head and threw it. Naked, she writhed closer and closer, beating her hips to me, crying out again and again in her carnal convulsions. I let her ride out her spasms, helping her achieve an even higher pleasure plateau before each orgasm with lips and fingers.

Her breasts half smothered me, the way she was rubbing them over my face. Her voice whispered, "I'm going back to school, Professor."

If she wanted to talk, that was fine by me. "Oh?" I said. "How come?"

"I intend to enroll in your L.S.D. courses. I'm going to take the whole works. I may even repeat the course, over and over."

Well, if that was what she wanted.

I turned my head sideways to breathe, nudging a breast out of the way. To my surprise, Lee Chi was standing beside us, lifting her quilted jacket off so her golden globes swung free to my stare.

"Now me," she giggled, pushing down her linen trousers.

"The controls," I yelled.

"They can take care of themselves. I tied the control rod with my sash. It's flying us straight and true for Hong Kong. The gas tank is almost full. We ought to land at Kai Tak airport before it runs out."

She came up behind Priscilla and put her smooth hands over those white breasts. Her own hard mounds pushed into

Priscilla's bare back. The widow cried out harshly as the scratching of those female appendages really got to her.

Lee Chi pulled Priscilla's head back and kissed her mouth. I think the widow went half out of her skull at that, I honestly don't believe she ever realized two girls could kiss each other that way. Neither of them were lesbian; this was just the cocktail before the main course.

Four hands and two mouths are better than my own alone. In seconds, Priscilla was jouncing crazily, sobbing and shuddering. We worked on her until she was a limp mass of quivering humanity. Then Lee Chi eased her off me and took her place.

Lee Chi attacked me as if there were no tomorrow. I didn't discourage her. I was having too good a time. I helped her climb her peaks as I had Priscilla Saunders. I told myself I was damn glad she was no robot.

"What are you going to do when you get to Hong Kong?" I wondered during a period of recovery from her orgasmic spasms.

"Go with you, be a student at your school."

"Good. But there isn't much I can teach you."

Lee Chi giggled and shook her head. "No, I am going to teach your people."

"What can you teach them?"

"How to make robots. What else?"

I was pretty dumb, I guess. I asked, "How?"

Lee Chi giggled, bouncing up and down on my inexhaustable jade stick. "I have been at the Robot Development Center a long time. I have even been able to copy some of the formulas those Russians used, plus a blueprint or two of their machines."

"They'll pay you a million dollars or more," I assured her, and she nodded happily. "But how did you sneak it out?"

Her eyes glanced sideways at Priscilla Saunders, who was staring down between her legs, watching the movement of our living parts. And they were really living, because the Chinese girl was bouncing and sliding around all over me.

Priscilla was goggle-eyed, and her mouth was open. Her somewhat heavy breasts were quite hard. They looked like big marble melons with the faint blue lines in them, tipped by the dark brown of her nipples. I honestly don't believe she heard a word that we were saying.

She was far too interested in what we were doing.

Lee Chi gasped between jounces, "You told me about Priscilla sewing those old scrolls inside her dress, remember? So when we were getting ready to leave, I sewed my papers and blueprints inside my jacket."

Her face was twisted in orgasmic ecstasy. She could not speak any more. She screwed her eyes shut, let her mouth fall open, and hung on with her fingernails buried in my shoulders.

Up and down and around, bounce and fall, she worked on and on. Her big breasts flopped and danced.

Behind her, Priscilla was licking her lips, staring at the Chinese doll. Her hands were quivering. As if to still them, she lifted them, put them on her swollen breasts. Her hips began working back and forth as if they held an invisible lover.

Staring at the newly made widow made me think of something, but I didn't know just what. She reminded me of someone, and I thought about that while Lee Chi bent her head so that her long black hair fell down about her face and wailed out her pleasure.

Damn! What *did* Priscilla remind me of?

Something important, something that was a part of this adventure. I stared at her, watched her open her eyes and lick her lips some more. She advanced on Lee Chi as if hynotized. Her hands slipped onto the sweat-wet sides of the golden girl and stroked them.

She began rubbing her white breasts on that yellow back, up and down and sideways. Her mouth came open, just as her moist palms slipped up to clasp and hold the heavy breasts that were shaking so crazily. Her hips beat the air.

The widow lady looked like a nympho.

Ah, that was it!

The blonde nympho whom I was to have banged in the Sheffield Inn, back in Uncle Sam land. Not that she looked anything like Cassie, though her actions were much the same. It was just that she was a hot white woman, I suppose, as Cassie had been.

Cassie was a loose end that I wanted to tie in with the rest of the action. I had the feeling that she was a part of it.

So my timing was off. I admit it. Priscilla was behind Lee Chi; her pale hands were under her breasts, lifting and shaking them; she was kissing the Chinese girl on her throat, pushing her tongue in her ear. She was one excited lady.

Nobody wanted to hear me ask questions.

Lee Chi was responding to the hands on her breasts and to the breasts rubbing up and down her back by going off on another orgasmic octave of sensation. I hesitated to ask the questions jumping around on the end of my tongue, so I waited.

Ever the gentleman.

The helicopter flew on through the skies of China. I marveled that it held so steady in the air, that it didn't go up and down, the way the girls were gyrating and jumping around. But we flew on and on.

Lee Chi screamed.

Priscilla Saunders was peering over her bare shoulder and watching her own hands tugging on the Chinese girl's stiff brown nipples, yanking them outward, adding a touch of pain to the pleasure I was giving the Chinese doll. She squeezed those breasts; she twisted them.

They were both panting like leaky bellows.

"Hey," I said plaintively. "I'd like to ask a question."

Some fat chance. I sat there and watched the girls get more and more excited. Priscilla had turned Lee Chi's head so she could kiss her, as the golden girl had done to her. I made a pretty good guess that widowhood was going to be the start of a new kind of life for Priscilla Saunders.

Then Lee Chi stiffened and panted out her release in perfumed gusts between Priscilla's open lips. Priscilla crooned to her, handling her breasts very tenderly.

"My turn now," the widow whispered.

"Oh, yes. Yes," Lee Chi agreed.

The white woman helped the yellow girl off me.

This was my chance. "Hey, I want to ask a question! Wait a second, girls. This is important."

Lee Chi staggered to the other side of the chopper, planted her soft behind to the wall and slid down to a sitting position. She had a silly, happy grin on her lips.

"Lee Chi!" I yelled.

She grinned at me. "Huh?"

"Did you ever make a white woman at the Robot Development Center?"

Priscilla Saunders was kneeling between my thighs. Her hands were stroking up and down, marveling at my phallic powers. She nuzzled me against her cheek. She put out her tongue and licked.

I said bravely, "Think, Lee Chi. Please, for my sake."

"I'd do anything for you," she vowed.

"A white woman. Her name was Cassie."

She sat there like a broken doll and thought. I could practically hear the wheels going around inside her head. Finally she nodded and grinned.

"Yes, I remember," she said, then sat up straighter, watching the widow.

Priscilla was holding me between both her fists, and she was using her teeth to nibble. Fear showed on Lee Chi's face.

"Don't bite," she screamed. "I'll want more when I get my strength back!"

That did it. I reached out and grabbed Mrs. Saunders by her long black hair and pushed her away. I said to her shocked face, "Wait, honey. Just wait until I get an answer to my question. It's really important."

She struggled, but weakly.

Lee Chi was on her feet, advancing on us both, the light of lust in her eyes. I said to her, "You hold it right there, baby. Answer me.

"This Cassie. Was she a robot too?"

Lee Chi nodded. "Oh, yes. Made from master model of lady correspondent in Peking. She was kidnapped and taken to the Robot Development Center. Novotny and Kolsikoff made fine duplicate of her. Very passionate girl. Needs men all the time. Like us." She giggled and gestured at Priscilla Saunders kneeling before me.

"Too bad about lady correspondent. She not lucky like me and you. They kill her when they get finished with her measurements. Very sad. Nobody glad to see her die. She was special favorite of Fedor Novotny."

She would be. I said, "What did they do with the robot who came to the Sheffield Inn? She wasn't there later on, after I'd killed the men she was with."

"I think the Red Chinese secret agents destroyed her. I

heard rumors. They got the bodies out of the motel and cleaned up the blood. Then they took the robot away."

"Were there any more copies of her?"

"All in the Robot Development Center. They must have burned in the fire."

Priscilla said, "How about it, Professor?"

She put her hands to mine and drew my fingers away from her hair. She leaned forward and began licking what her hands were still holding. Lee Chi watched, very interested, nodding her head from time to time as if in approval of her technique.

Satisfied that I was having fun, the Chinese girl put one bare foot on the seat where I was sitting. She rose upward, and put her other foot beyond my further thigh, so that she was spraddled over me.

"Any more questions?" she asked.

I started shaking my head just as Priscilla Saunders started to giggle. I looked down at her.

"What's with you?" I asked.

"I was just thinking that we ought to form our own air line in and out of Red China. Our motto could be, 'You'll love, flying with us.' "

Lee Chi sat down. Priscilla leaned forward.

We loved, flying—all the way to Hong Kong.

www.ingramcontent.com/pod-product-compliance
Ingram Content Group UK Ltd.
Pitfield, Milton Keynes, MK11 3LW, UK
UKHW022255280225
455674UK00001B/34